BREAKING SILENCE

L.M. HALLORAN

COPYRIGHT

*For the broken hearts that keep beating
and those strong enough to love them.*

PROLOGUE

I love a good horror film. Bring on the gore and make it realistic. I'm not squeamish in the slightest. With two younger siblings I helped my mom raise, I've dealt with my fair share of bodily byproducts, too.

But this... this is making me queasy.

Maybe because it wasn't kids that made this mess, but grown-ass humans.

Kelly's mutters of disgust mirror the sentiments in my head as she cleans on the opposite side of the massive living room. Something pink appears in my peripheral as she waves it in my direction.

"Look at this, Sophie!"

Taking a break from mopping vomit off hardwood floors, I look. And promptly wish I hadn't. There's a giant dildo in her—thankfully gloved—hand.

Weak sunlight filters through the windows behind her, catching and refracting subtly off the pink rubber. "What's that all over it?"

Her face scrunches as she examines it. "Looks like glitter. Jesus, I really hope no one..." She trails off, then shakes her head. "You know the only thing I hate about these kinds of jobs?"

My lips twitch at the abrupt shift, which is a staple of her personality. "Scooping shit out of pools?"

She considers, then shakes her head. "That only happened one time. What I really hate is that these jobs break my pink glasses, ya know? Celebrity parties are a different level of gross. It's like money and fame turn them into rabid animals, and booze and drugs unchain them."

I smirk. "I think you mean rose-colored glasses."

"Whatever, yeah." She tosses the dildo into the giant black trash bag beside her, then looks at her watch. "I'll finish up in here if you want to start on the bedrooms."

"You sure?" I ask, glancing from the half-cleaned vomit to bottles on every surface, cigarette butts in plants, a suspicious dark stain on one wall, and a pillow smeared with what had better be whipped cream.

I'm sure the people here last night thought it was a great party, but from this side of things, it looks like an advertisement for rehab.

She grins at me. "Of course. The bedrooms are usually worse."

I huff out a laugh. "Rude."

Call me naïve, but I'm not sure how much worse the bedrooms can be. It's not like I'm going to use a black light or anything, and I'll be wearing gloves.

"You know my favorite part about this job, though?" Kelly asks as I'm stripping off my gloves for a fresh pair.

I lift my carryall of cleaning supplies. "What's that?"

"The money, honey."

We share a grin of complete agreement, though mine fades fast as I turn and head down the hall.

Kelly is paid extremely well, and she deserves every penny. While I've been locked into rotating, multiple-job hell the last two years since graduating college, Kelly went after what she wanted right out of high school. She built her company, Kelly Executive Cleaning, from unfailing tenacity and hard work, and has made a name for herself in the right circles.

Kelly would say she owes her success to simple luck

—being in the right place at the right time. When she was a struggling twenty-year-old trying to make ends meet, she received a call from a panicking teenager who'd found her cleaning service on Yelp. That teenager happened to be the son of Audrey Fitz, Academy Award winning actress, and he'd been panicking because he'd thrown a party that got out of hand and had trashed his parents' house while they were out of town.

A one-woman army, Kelly had made his problem go away; at least, the destroyed house part. The kid had forgotten about security videos, which caught some, if not all, of the insanity that night. He'd also forgotten that his parents monitored his bank account. Two days later, Kelly received a call from Audrey herself. She'd seen both the damage and the aftermath and had been seriously impressed.

The rest was history.

These days, Kelly has five employees on her payroll. In addition to her team having steady work at upscale residences and businesses around Seattle, she's personally on speed dial for some of the biggest names—or rather, their lackeys—in finance, tech, sports, and entertainment.

When the rich throw parties, especially in rented houses, Kelly makes it look like they never happened.

The only reason *I'm* here is because we were together last night, enjoying margaritas at our favorite Mexican place, when a call came in from a harried PA whose client needed immediate cleaning in the morning. The offered price: $400/hr.

With a gleam in her eye, Kelly had accepted, then promptly told me I'd be joining her. When I'd laughed her off, she'd said "pretty please" with a face I couldn't resist, then told me her other staff were all booked, the house was three-thousand square feet, and she didn't want to do it alone... and I'd take home a thousand dollars for five hours of work. When I still wasn't completely swayed, she said she'd pay me under the table.

There were a million other things I could, *should*, be doing on my only day off this week, but she knew—and I knew, even though she'd never rub it in my face—that I needed the money more than I needed to catch up on sleep and errands.

Sighing, I stretch my already sore back and trudge upstairs and down a dim hallway to the closed double doors at the end, figuring I might as well start with the biggest room and work my way back.

My mind floating between where the money will go —bills first, the rest to my mom—I push open the doors and blink into the darkness. I fumble on the wall for a switch but come up empty. Shifting to allow ambient light from the hallway past me, I spy the distinct outline of a bed and a nightstand with a lamp.

Despite my brain informing me the master suite, while obscenely large and dark, is empty of threats, my heart rate doesn't care. For a few seconds, I consider fetching my cell phone from downstairs and using the flashlight to find a light switch. I also eye the distant curtains—blackout, floor-to-ceiling—but making the trek to them feels impossible. Not to mention I'd still need to find a light even with them opened. Despite the midmorning hour, the February sky is dark with Seattle's latest winter storm.

Suck it up, idiot. You're being ridiculous. You're not some weak, snivelly kid.

The pep talk isn't effective, and my panting has fogged up my glasses. I take gulps of air that thankfully don't make me gag. Faint alcohol fumes mix with an even fainter hint of oceany cologne. No vomit, at least.

You can do this. Go, go, go.

I drop my supplies by the door and force my feet to walk fast toward the closest side of the bed. My eyesight continues to adjust, proving what a loser I am: the room is clearly uninhabited and not even that messy. There are some blobs on the floor that I'm guessing are clothes and shoes, and the king bed's comforter is piled up on one side. The main debauchery definitely took place downstairs.

My fingers fumble with the lamp, but I can barely feel anything through my cleaning gloves. My glasses slip down my nose. With a huff of annoyance, I strip off my gloves and continue my search for the elusive switch. There's no little plastic dial at the bottom of the bulb, no switch around the square base.

I should have gone for the damn curtains.

"Fucking rich people lamps," I mutter, running my fingers down the chord, trying to find a rotating mechanism.

Then I hear it. A rustle of bedding right beside me.

I freeze.

My neck cracks as I turn my head toward the bed. My sight is abruptly enhanced—*thanks, adrenaline*—and I see the white comforter move. As I watch, a muscled, tattooed arm snakes out from beneath it and reaches for me.

My muscles tremble, unwilling to obey my commands to run. I can hear my breath, harsh and panting, but my mind is oddly quiet. *Fawn response,* some deep, rational part of me observes.

A tanned hand moves closer, fingers searching, reminding me of Thing from The Addams Family. A tiny squeak escapes my throat as it finds my hip, sealing onto me like a monstrous suction cup.

"There you are," comes a deep, sleepy rumble.

The rest happens fast.

The comforter lifts and so does the beast beneath it. I'm tugged forward, a thick arm snaking around my ass, another hand spinning me in place. A second later, I'm hauled into hot darkness, my back to his front.

There's too much of him, too much happening—the searing rope of his arm around my middle, his legs rising beneath mine, the distinct press of an erection against my ass.

It's my worst nightmare come true.

"Why're you dressed?" he murmurs, thrusting gently against me. Another squeak bypasses my closed throat as warm lips find my bare neck beneath my ponytail. He breathes deeply, then stiffens into an unmoving rock behind me.

"Julia?" His voice is clear now. Awake.

All I can do is shake my head.

"Fuck!" He scrambles backward, all the way across the bed. There's a huge thump as he falls off the side and hits the floor.

My muscles finally unlock and I gasp, then rocket off the bed and sprint for the door. Tears of relief bead in my eyelashes.

His raised voice floats after me. "Oh my God! Wait—I'm sorry! Who are you? What the fuck is happening right now!"

I fly down the stairs and don't stop running until I reach the kitchen, where Kelly is loading the dishwasher. She glances up at me as I round the island and the blood drains from her face.

"Jesus, Soph! Are you all right? What happened?" She grabs my arms. Her mouth keeps moving, but I can't hear her over the dull roar in my ears and the crashing of my nervous system. All I can do is shake my head and point over my shoulder.

She looks up and stills, her gaze locked on the entrance to the kitchen, at a height I numbly realize means *he* must be standing there.

"I'm so sorry," he says, deep voice dripping with remorse. "It was dark. I thought she was my girlfriend. *Fuck*. What can I do? Is she okay? Who even are you people? Did Phil hire you?"

Kelly's expression turns nuclear as it shifts back to me. "What did he do?" Her voice is calm, but rage burns in her eyes.

I swallow and force out, "Nothing. Honest. He just surprised me."

She scans my face, my hair, then takes stock of the state of my clothes. What she sees, coupled with how long I was gone, softens the dangerous glint in her eyes. With a firm but gentle hand, she guides me behind her. I'm four inches taller than her, but her show of protection makes something in me relax.

"Our apologies, Mr. Sullivan," she says with false cheer. "We were contacted last night and given the code to get in. Obviously, we were under the impression no one would be here."

I feel his eyes on me, and I can't help glancing up. I almost choke at the sight: he's just as tall as I thought, around six-four, and tattooed liberally from his neck to his feet. Dark, intricate ink meets the waistband of his black boxers, which do absolutely fuck-all to obscure the natural size of what's beneath them. My eyeballs burn and I jerk my gaze back up to mussed blond hair and a face that is known the world-over since his band's rise to superstardom four years ago.

Matt Sullivan.

Lead guitarist for the indie rock sensation, Breaking Giants.

Smoky blue eyes sear mine. "Are you really okay?"

I nod, a jerk of my head.

His attention shifts to Kelly. "Give me five minutes to get dressed and I'll get out of your hair." His gaze flickers back to me, snagging on the dark ponytail draped over my shoulder. Suddenly, his voice lowers and hardens. "Are we cool? Or do I need to call a lawyer?"

Kelly bristles but glances at me. "It's up to you."

"No," I whisper, then say more clearly, "No." I can't seem to look at him, so I focus on Kelly. "It was my fault."

She opens her mouth, but *he* speaks first.

"The hell it was."

I'm so surprised by the impassioned tone of his voice that I look at him with wide eyes. His nostrils flare like he's angry, but oddly, I somehow know that whatever he's feeling has nothing to do with me, but rather with my reaction to him.

He takes a deep breath, his voice gentling, "I'm really sorry I scared you. You did nothing wrong. The room was dark. You thought no one was there, and I'm the asshole who grabbed you." He pauses. "You can kick me in the balls if you want."

I blink. Kelly snorts.

Matt smiles, a slow grin full of mischief and challenge that makes his eyes sparkle and transforms him from some ethereal superstar into someone *real.* My lips twitch involuntarily in response.

"Thanks, but that won't be necessary," I manage, my voice still weak but firm.

"Okay, well, the offer stands if we ever run into each

other again. Sorry again. I'll leave through the garage. Give me five." He turns and strides away, giving us an eyeful of his muscled back and its large, unfinished tattoo, a vibrant waterscape: stormy skies and sea, a Viking longboat, sea serpent, sirens on rocks...

A tattoo I recognize.

Because I drew it.

1

PRESENT DAY

"*D*o you have any idea how long I've waited for this?"

I roll my eyes and settle back onto the tattoo bench, adjusting the pillow under my head until I'm comfortable. My right arm is stretched over a padded surface perpendicular to my body, and my brother Josh stares down at my blank inner bicep like it's gold.

"Quit drooling and get to work," I tell him on a yawn. "My shift starts at one."

He laughs, floppy brown hair covering his eyes before he tosses it back. I tune out the familiar sounds of him prepping his workspace and scroll through social media, not really paying attention because I'm tired as hell.

I'm also hungover, which is one of the absolute worst things to be when getting inked. Alcohol dehydrates you and thins the blood, which makes for a painful and messy session. I've been chugging Gatorade since my alarm blasted me awake at nine, but it's probably too little too late.

Normally, I'd never drink the night before a tattoo, but yesterday was my twenty-ninth birthday. Kelly would have murdered me if I'd refused to go out. Plus, my big brother is one of the most in-demand tattoo artists in Seattle—booked years in advance—and this appointment has been on his calendar for five years. Not because he wouldn't have squeezed me in before now, but because of a dumb, drunk promise made ten years ago yesterday that if we were both still alive in a decade, he'd get to tattoo whatever he wanted on me.

I'm expecting something ridiculous like a cat licking itself or a heart with his name in it, but I honestly don't care. Our mom would throw a fit if I told her that—she can barely stomach the fact her two oldest children are tattooed—but it's the truth. Josh and I share a similar worldview. Some of our common ideologies are: sometimes art doesn't have to mean anything, and we don't care what our skin will look like when we're eighty.

As per our agreement, I don't look as Josh smooths on a stencil and carefully pulls up the paper to leave the temporary purple lines. When he's satisfied, the testing buzz of the gun tickles my ears and senses.

"Ready?"

I grunt and toss my phone into the black hole of my purse. "Don't sound so happy about it."

He laughs and bends over my arm. A warm, gloved hand stretches the skin to find his perfect canvas. Then he gets to work. The pain isn't pleasant, but within a few minutes, my mind goes to the soft, fuzzy place it does every time I get tattooed. I'm asleep a few minutes after that.

However long later, I wake up as Josh wipes a paper towel over my tender skin.

I blink up at him, still half-asleep. "That's it?"

He sits back, placing his gun on the tray beside him and pulling off his gloves, then levels me with a look that's half-admiring and half-sad. He doesn't have to say anything because I know what he's thinking. The only people who fall asleep under the needle are those with capital T trauma.

Sitting up, I stretch my legs and lift my arm to see what he permanently marked me with. As soon as my brain takes in the design, my eyes well with tears. It stretches from just under my armpit midway down my bicep—all the free space available on the cluttered canvas of my arm.

The man is famous for a reason, and the intricate lines, colors, and shading are perfect. He didn't have a lot of space to work with, but the details are insane. A pigtailed little girl sits on a tree swing, one foot angled toward the ground like she's kicking dirt. The realism is incredible, from her fingers wrapped around rope to the barely-there expression on her downturned face. The tree above her is gnarled and old, dropping glistening orange and red leaves that swirl around in an imaginary breeze.

"Shit, Joshy. I was expecting a poop emoji."

He barks a laugh. "Fuck you. You know I wouldn't do you dirty like that."

I blink rapidly, then meet his dark green eyes, identical to mine. "Thanks."

He nods, his smile soft, then cleans and covers the tattoo in a derma shield. "Leave it on for four days or until it falls off. If it starts to leak—"

"Yeah, yeah," I interrupt him. "This isn't my first rodeo. Did I bleed more than usual?"

"Eh, not that I noticed. But I can smell the fumes coming out of your skin. How was the birthday celebration?"

My mind flashes back to strobing lights, thumping

music, and Kelly, Pamela, and Juliette squealing in my face.

"Kelly dragged me to that new club on South Washington." I yawn again, my jaw cracking. "I felt like a grandma."

Josh laughs. "You still got carded, though, didn't you?"

I chuckle and nod. We're both cursed with genetics that refuse to align our faces with our ages. Slipping off the table, I reach for my purse. "You free for dinner Wednesday?" I ask as I sling it over my shoulder.

"Maybe." He looks up from where he's cleaning his tray. "As long as you're not cooking."

"Har har, asshole. We'll order in."

A faint beeping comes from the front door of the studio as someone keys in the code. I glance behind me as the door opens, then blanch at the sight of who walks through. My stomach drops. My palms start sweating. Before the man can turn his head and see me, I blurt, "Call me later," to Josh and power walk past the man, my head down and face angled away.

As the heavy glass closes slowly behind me, I hear a familiar voice ask, "Who was that?" There's a pause in which I imagine Josh's answer. Then a laugh-filled question, "Why does she hate me?"

"Must be your ugly face," answers my brother laconically.

There's a low laugh just before the door closes and cuts the sound off.

THREE HOURS LATER, as I transfer clean mugs from a crate onto the shelf behind the espresso machines, I try not to dwell on that voice or the fact Josh didn't warn me he had the appointment after mine. Which I recognize is a crazy thought in and of itself, because my brother has no idea about my history with the lead guitarist of Breaking Giants.

Then again, the chances Matt Sullivan even remembers the twenty-three-year-old maid he accidentally groped are next to nil. It's been six years and I look completely different. I didn't have many tattoos then, and my hair is back to its natural golden brown from the black it was. No more glasses, either; it took me a while to pay off my LASIK surgery, but I have no regrets.

I doubt Matt gave me a second thought once he left that morning. His fame and fortune have only grown since then, and so has the trail of weeping women he's left behind. Last I heard, though, he was engaged and settling down. The wedding is next March—I might have read the online article three times. The lucky bride is a gorgeous woman named Melody who he's been with for a couple of years. They look great together. Happy.

There's absolutely zero reason he should have any effect on me whatsoever.

The fact I've followed his career with interest, that I usually end up Googling pictures of him when I'm lonely or drunk, or that I occasionally have flashbacks of what those seconds in his arms felt like—minus the terror of the actual event, of course... none of it means anything. I do not, nor have I ever, had a crush on Matt Sullivan. I'm twenty-nine, not nineteen. Way too old to be obsessed with a thirty-something rock star who's getting married.

Stupid. So stupid.

A pair of legging-clad legs appears in my peripheral. "What did those mugs ever do to you?" asks my co-manager, Allison, with a teasing smile.

I wince and focus on placing the final three mugs carefully, with minimal clanking. Standing, I swipe damp hair off my forehead. August in Seattle is as fickle as I am when I'm PMS'ing. Sometimes mellow, sometimes ready to light shit on fire. The last few days are firmly in the latter category, and Tullamore Café's doors and windows are all open, the overhead fans working hard and doing next to nothing to combat the heat.

If someone had asked me ten years ago if I thought I'd be happy managing a funky café in Fremont full-time, I'd have laughed in their face. I had pipe dreams of being a famous artist, traveling the world, and making bank doing what I loved. But life—rent, bills, student loans—hammered out the arrogance of my youth.

I am, in fact, happy most days. More than that, I know how lucky I am. The owner, Owen Griffiths, is amazing to work for, though he stepped back from the day-to-day business last year, leaving Allison and me in charge. Thankfully, the two of us mesh well, and our staff is like an extended family. I have a weekend off every month, and since I work as the closing manager, I can sleep in most days. I am *not* a morning person.

"You heading out?" I ask Allison, glancing at the large clock stationed above our chalkboard menu.

She nods. "Brian will be here in a few to take over for Jack, and Grey and Dania will be here at five to close with you and help with open mic night. You've got Harry in the kitchen until eight. I also called three more A/C companies. Cross your fingers someone calls back." She grimaces. "Although I'm not holding my breath. The last place said they're booked solid for the next two months."

I groan. "I told you we should have had it serviced in

February. By the time summer hits, it's too late for an appointment."

She winces. "I know. My bad." She glances at the half-full café and the customer Jack is handling at the register. "At least business is steady."

"Amen to that."

She turns, then swivels back. "You're still coming tomorrow night, right?"

"What? Where?"

She sighs with exaggerated affront. "You have the weekend off, and it happens to be *the* weekend we're playing this month!"

"Sorry, still not picking up what you're putting down."

"Disco bowling!" she hollers, earning curious looks from customers and a laugh from Jack, who's currently making an iced drink a few feet away.

"Disco bowling is still a thing? Aren't we a little old for that?" At the look on her face, I laugh. "I'm just messing with you. Of course I'm coming. I promised, didn't I?"

Allison cackles. "You did."

"Then I'll be there. You probably won't want me on your team, though." I point to my right arm and the bandage. "This is going to be sore tomorrow for sure."

She waves off my unsubtle attempt to back out. "No

one cares about winning, anyway. It'll be fun. You'll see." She grins conspiratorially. "Besides, I talked to Rose earlier. She and Julian are coming, which means there's a good chance the rest of the band will show up, too. Including *you know who*."

Ah, fuck.

Rose is Owen's cousin and former co-owner of Tullamore; she sold him her half of the business last year for a whopping fifteen dollars. Julian is *the* Julian Ashburn, lead singer of Breaking Giants and Rose's husband of two years.

"Nope. No way."

I shake my head adamantly, filled with regret for the night a couple years ago when Allison and I shared a bottle of wine on my couch and I told her about my *not-crush* on Matt Sullivan.

"You promised," she reminds me with a glint in her eye. Then she leans toward me, her voice lowering to a whisper. "It isn't news yet, but it will be sometime next week, so I don't feel bad about telling you. The wedding was called off a few months ago." There's a dramatic pause wherein her wide, sparkling eyes meet mine. "He's back on the market, Sophie."

2

He's back on the market.

The words tumble in my head until around six-thirty, when there's a substantial uptick in customers as people start spilling in for open mic night. Brian and Dania work to move tables and adjust chairs. Customers help them, laughing and jockeying for prime seats. Despite the energy-sucking heat of the day, the mood is light and boisterous.

Grey and I handle drinks—almost exclusively iced—while Dania handles the clipboard with tonight's acts. The lights in the café dim as the ones over the stage brighten. The first act, a kid with a guitar who looks no older than my sister, takes the stage. He's confident, though, and when he starts playing, it's evident why. The crowd loves him.

Eventually, the line for drinks and bakery items shortens and ends. I send Grey on a break as Brian resumes register duties, then make myself an iced tea and meander toward the front door. Leaning a hip on the end of the counter, I bob my head along to Kid Genius's impressive guitar skills and pray for a breeze.

Instead of a breeze, I get my brother in all his floppy-haired, shit-eating grin glory.

My mouth drops. "Joshy! What are you doing here?"

He laughs. "I just finished up with the client after you. I mentioned you've been telling me to stop by forever, so we came over."

My fingers and toes go numb as another figure turns the corner outside and walks through the door. He smacks my brother on the back and looks around, gaze scanning the crowded space, the musician currently on stage, and finally swinging all the way around to...

I pin my attention on my brother's face, ignoring the pressure I feel on my own from someone else's. "What do you want to drink? On the house." I manage the barest glance in Matt's direction. "For both of you, obviously."

"Whatever. Something cold," says my brother, who I suddenly want to smack into next week. "You got the drinks, man? I'll see if I can get some seats."

"Sounds good," comes the mild reply.

Then my brother—now my worst enemy—meanders toward the stage, leaving me alone with *him*.

I move down the counter, grateful for the barrier. *He* follows, a blond giant in the corner of my eye. Grabbing a couple of glasses, I dump ice into them, spilling more than a few cubes on the rubber mat under my feet.

"Any preference?" I ask in the direction of the person I refuse to look at. Unfortunately, my erratically swinging gaze means I glance down and see the coffee stain on my white tank top, which only reminds me that my hair is a hot mess piled on my head and my cut-off shorts are damp from sweat beneath my dirty half-apron. At least the lights are dimmer than usual.

"Do I have something on my face?" he asks abruptly, laughter in his voice.

Fuck, Sophie. Grow up.

Sucking air through my nose, I force myself to look at him. At his nose, specifically, which is sadly just as perfect as the rest of him.

"Nope. Sorry. Just, err..." Heavily tattooed arms brace on the counter opposite me, derailing my fumbling reply and sending me back to that morning he doesn't remember and I still think about too often.

"If you want an autograph or something, just ask," he says softly. "I don't bite."

There's no arrogance in his voice, just acceptance

and a bit of tiredness, which only makes it worse. He thinks I'm a super fan, overwhelmed by his celebrity. This probably happens to him all the damn time.

I mean, I love Breaking Giants as much as the next Millennial, and Matt's an incredible guitarist, but I'm not a groupie or anything. My stupid obsession is unrelated. But there's no way I can explain it without sounding like a nutcase.

In the end, I just stare at him, my muscles frozen, my throat swollen closed. Clearly, my go-to physiological response when overwhelmed, though notably, it hasn't happened to this level since *that day*.

"You're Josh's little sister, right? You were at his studio this morning." A hand extends to me over the counter; I stare at it like it's a cobra about to strike. His voice turns teasing. "I'm Matt. Just a normal guy. It's nice to meet you."

The café breaks into applause, jarring and loud. My head finally pops out of my ass, and I realize I'm being a total jerk. Matt's hand falters, dropping toward his side. I grab it before it's too far to reach and give him a firm shake.

Calluses.

Strong, long fingers.

I let go after two seconds. Clearing my throat, I look

into his eyes. The low lighting makes their blue turn gray, and I hope it also camouflages my red cheeks.

"It's nice to meet you, too," I manage to get out in a mostly normal voice. "Sorry. It's been a long day. I'm probably a little ink sick." It's a lie—I feel fine except for this unholy effect he has on me. The only time I've felt the weird, flu-like symptoms of too much ink too fast was after sitting for a six-hour session on my back.

As an afterthought, I add, "I'm Sophie."

He grins; my breath hitches. "All good. And I've known your name for years. Josh is the only chatty tattoo artist I know, but he's so good I keep coming back in spite of his annoying voice."

A startled laugh escapes me, which only makes his grin widen. He nods toward my arms. "A fellow glutton for punishment, I see."

While I don't have traditional tattoo sleeves—one interwoven design shoulder to wrist—there isn't a lot of space that doesn't have something. Patchwork, I've heard it called. Matt's ink is the same, though his tattoos are bolder, his canvas a lot larger than mine.

I can't stop my mouth from asking, "What did you work on today?"

"My back," he says, then shudders. "I've been trying to get this thing finished for seven years, but it's the one place on my body that makes me cry like a baby. At least it's finally almost done."

I laugh. "I've heard the back is really painful for some people."

His eyes narrow, smile softening. "Not for you, though, I'm guessing?"

A frisson of awareness skates up my spine. I remind myself there's no way on the planet that he knows what's on my back, or even that it's tattooed.

Does he know I drew what's on his? Did Josh tell him?

My brother is an incredible artist, but we have slightly different styles. After doing several iterations based on Matt's requests that weren't quite what he was looking for, Josh had asked me in a rare show of nerves to sketch the design. He'd been fairly new in his career at that point and had told me only that the client was famous.

Knowing how important it could be for Josh's career, I'd done the drawing gladly. In fact, it remained one of my favorite pieces to date. I still had the original in my apartment.

I hadn't known who'd received my art until that fateful Saturday morning six years ago.

"Nah," I answer him with a small smile. "I fall asleep under the needle. My back was done in a couple of long naps."

Matt laughs, a hand swiping over his stubbled jaw before he leans a hip on the counter. "Lucky you." His head cocks toward the stage, his eyes following to latch onto a female performer singing and playing guitar. "She's not bad." His gaze veers back to me. "I haven't been down here in so long. You weren't working here three years ago, were you?"

"Nope."

His eyes trail over my face, up to my hair, and briefly down my body. Little fires start everywhere his gaze touches. "I didn't think so. I would have remembered you."

My heart trips, then pounds at my ribs like they're a door and it wants out. I laugh awkwardly; it sounds strangled. *Is he hitting on me?* Impossible. *Right?*

"I've only been here about a year," I say quickly. "I was working at a competitor and Owen recruited me. I'm the night manager."

Matt continues staring at me with unnerving focus. So naturally, I continue babbling like I'm a middle schooler at my first dance.

"Josh wanted me to apprentice with him—we both majored in Fine Arts—but believe it or not, I have an aversion to needles. Not having them used on me, obviously, but the idea of using them on someone else freaks me out. So no tattooing."

"What's your medium of art?" he asks, leaning a little closer as the music gets louder.

"Pencil mostly. And charcoal. I do, uh, mostly portraiture and realism. Some fantasy, some water scenes. Depends on my mood. That's one of mine." I nod to the wall by the front door and breathe a sigh of relief when he walks over to look at it.

A second later, relief morphs to panic as I realize it's not too dissimilar from what's on his back—sirens on rocks, shattered and sinking ship nearby.

Oh, fuck.

Will he recognize the style?

No way. It's too dark.

I make a mental note to pull the art tomorrow, so there's no chance of him seeing it if he ever comes back.

Suddenly, Matt stiffens. He spins on a heel and pins me to the spot with his narrowed gaze.

I freeze, unblinking, until someone else moves into my line of sight, blocking Matt from view. "Yo, Soph, what's the holdup on drinks?"

My brother is no longer my worst enemy. In fact, he's been promoted to my favorite person on Earth.

3

"Absolutely not," I say for the tenth time.

"Come on," whines my sister, her voice at a pitch that makes me wince. "I'm almost eighteen."

I scoff. "Nice try, Beks."

I was ten when my little brother Patrick was born, and Beka came along three years later. Their dad, my stepfather, bailed shortly after her birth because he's a weak piece of shit who couldn't handle the fact his baby girl wasn't perfect. We haven't heard from him since.

At nine days old, Beka was diagnosed with an atrial septal defect in her heart. Basically, there was a small hole where there definitely shouldn't be one. As if that wasn't enough to scare my mom half to death, Beka also had two *other* heart defects that likewise hadn't been detectable during pregnancy.

Her first open heart surgery was at ten days old. Her second—and hopefully her last—was just after her first birthday.

She's fifteen now, turning sixteen in three weeks. Hair a touch darker than mine, with eyes between blue and green, she's a knockout. And though she won't be running any marathons or jumping out of airplanes in her lifetime, and has to monitor her condition carefully, she's a mostly normal teenager.

And therefore a giant pain in my ass.

"And Mom would kill us," I continue. "Do you even care about our lives?"

She scowls at me, then turns to Josh. In an instant, her expression morphs into what we call her Disney Princess face: pouting lips, big eyes beseeching and a little bit crazy.

From across the table, Josh watches us blearily over his mug of coffee. Saturday morning breakfast at our mom's house is a longstanding tradition we rarely break, even when violently hungover like he is right now. Apparently, he and Matt went bar hopping after their stint at Tullamore last night and he didn't get home until four o'clock this morning.

Since I found out twenty minutes ago, I've had to bite my tongue on stupid questions. Like whether or not Matt said anything about me or the tattoo on his back.

Thanks to Josh's interruption last night, I'd avoided answering the question blazing from Matt's eyes as I'd swiftly made them Italian Sodas. And thanks to a group of customers walking in the door right after and immediately recognizing Matt—and mobbing him for selfies—I'd managed to avoid him altogether the rest of the evening. Busy with work, I hadn't even seen them leave.

"Tell her, Josh," I demand.

His half-open eye twitches. "I'm not tattooing you, Beks."

She deflates into sullenness, Disney turning into Depeche Mode. I almost smile.

The front door opens and closes, and a few seconds later, Patrick waltzes in, his girlfriend, Bronx, in tow. At nineteen and blessed with a heartbreaking face, our younger brother is full of swagger and bad ideas—like dating a woman named Bronx, who's seven years older with an ex-husband in prison.

But we love him anyway.

Greetings and small talk ensue. Beka and I side-eye each other knowingly as Bronx flirts with Josh right in front of Patrick. Both men are oblivious, Josh because he's hungover and Patrick because he can't comprehend any woman not worshipping him completely.

"I'm gonna help Mom," I murmur to Beka.

She nods, eyes pinned on the disaster in front of her like she's watching reality TV. I escape to the kitchen.

"Oh, good," says my mom as I push through the door. She blows a strand of brown hair out of her eyes and smiles. "You can help me carry everything out."

No matter how many times Josh and I have offered to help her cook Saturday mornings, Marjorie Marshall always refuses our help. We think it's because she feels guilty that our teen years were overwhelmed by helping her raise Patrick and Beka while she worked two jobs.

She has no idea how amazing we think she is, even though we tell her as much as we can. Neither of us has ever resented the time we spent babysitting our siblings instead of doing 'normal' teen stuff. As we were both nerdy art kids, sports and after-school activities weren't our thing, anyway. Neither was house parties, racing cars, tagging, or any of the other reckless shit kids our age got into.

It's easy to acknowledge now that our commitment at home most nights and weekends likely kept us out of trouble. A lot of our school friends—outcasts and oddballs like us—ended up on dark roads by junior year.

None of that saved me when I moved out, however, just delayed it until the last year of art school. I'd barely graduated. Josh, on the other hand—like Kelly—

managed to stay on the straight road. Together, they were the lighthouse I eventually managed to swim toward.

I like to think of those dark days as a sunken ship that smashed against rocks and will never sail again.

After giving my mom a kiss on her soft cheek and murmuring my thanks, I grab a plate piled high with pancakes, another with scrambled eggs, then make my way back into the dining room. I return for plates and utensils. Mom passes me with condiments and napkins, her happy, soothing voice joining the chatter. It's a familiar song, one that settles my nerves and grounds me in the moment.

Even when the world is spiraling around me, I always have my family.

BY THE TIME Saturday evening rolls around, my family-induced glow is gone. I've spent the last hour praying for a sudden bout of food poisoning or the flu. No such luck.

Backdoor Billiards & Bowl on a weekend night is not my kind of scene. Not only do I suck at bowling, I'm burnt out on loud music and the club aesthetic I can see going on behind tinted windows. After the club on

Thursday, my nightlife quota for the year has been met. My head already hurts just thinking about black lights, strobing disco balls, and trying not to embarrass myself throwing a giant ball at pins.

But I promised.

As I approach the doors and see the **Closed for Private Event** sign, my nerves ramp up even further. No way Allison got the entire place shut down for her monthly bowling meetup—which means she was telling the truth. There are famous people inside.

Please, don't let him *be here.*

My breath trips each time it passes over the pulse pounding in my throat. I swipe clammy palms on my jeans, wishing for the thousandth time that I didn't take promises seriously—and that Allison hadn't called this afternoon and made me swear to stay at least an hour before I bailed.

As I stall outside, I eyeball the giant dude standing just inside the door, figuring he's security. Maybe Allison forgot to put my name on the list?

A girl can dream.

Footsteps to my right draw my focus to a curvy woman with short pink hair booking it down the side-walk toward me. When she spots me, she grins and squeals, running for me with her arms outstretched. I've only met Allison's girlfriend, Katie, a handful of times, but each time, she's greeted me like we're lifelong friends. With her bubbly personality and genuine good humor, she's impossible not to like.

I'm not usually a hugger, but I return her embrace with relief. At least I won't be walking in alone.

"Oh my gosh, I'm so glad you came." She grins and grabs my arm, all but hauling me toward the door. "Of all the nights your schedule finally matched up with our monthly game, huh? Talk about overwhelming." She giggles. "My girlfriend has famous friends. I'm so glad someone else was late, too. I came straight from work."

With zero hesitation, she pulls open the door. Thumping music spills outside, a blend of house and disco that thankfully isn't loud enough to make any ears bleed.

The security guy smiles and asks, "Here for the private party?"

Katie nods excitedly. "Katie Zimmer and Sophie Marshall."

He checks the list in his hand, then gestures toward the group of people clustered around the last few lanes. "Head on over. Have fun, ladies."

I only hear about a word out of every three Katie says on the way to the group, because I'm preoccupied with scanning faces as we get closer.

Matt isn't here, which is a relief.

And also, if I'm honest with myself, a little bit of a disappointment.

The rest of the band is present. Julian Ashburn, Nick Henderson, and Jackson Everett. Julian and Nick are with their wives, and Jackson is with a woman who I assume is his girlfriend or date since she's sitting on his lap. Allison's normal crew is here, too, four women and two men, all of whom are trying really hard to play it cool with the rock stars in the vicinity.

Allison spots us and waves excitedly, breaking away from her conversation to head toward us. Katie abandons me to meet her halfway while I walk at a slower pace.

It's then, as I scan the congregation one more time, noticing body language and social cues, that I realize I'm the only person here without a partner.

Dammit, Allison.

"Fancy meeting you here," murmurs a familiar voice behind me. Sexy and dark. A little taunting. A lot overwhelming.

I spin and look up at Matt's grinning face.

4

I glance quickly behind him, toward the door, but the space is empty. He's alone.

"What are you looking for?" he asks, lips twitching. "Or are you considering an escape plan?"

"Definitely escape," I answer, and he chuckles.

I pivot to see Allison and Katie looking at us with glee. Others are watching, too, most notably Julian and Rose. Neither is smiling, which gives me a weird crawly feeling. I've met Rose a few times at Tullamore; I'm sure she recognizes me.

Then I remember why Matt is alone—he's not getting married anymore. I make the appropriate logical leap and assume that his ex-fiancée was friends with Rose. Which means she thinks...

I bite my lip on a hysterical laugh.

Electric awareness slides down my back as Matt steps closer. "Come on, I'll introduce you."

He doesn't touch me, but the forward motion of his body doesn't give me much room to maneuver away from where he's guiding me. I can't exactly run toward Allison without looking like an idiot. I'm not sure she'd be much help, anyway, since she hasn't stopped grinning evilly at me.

Conversations die as Matt successfully herds me before his bandmates and friends, all of them standing or sitting on lounge furniture around the ball return.

When Matt's arm settles heavily on my shoulders, I instinctively flinch. He murmurs, "Relax, Dollface," then says loudly, "Hey, guys, this is my new friend, Sophie. She's Josh Marshall's little sister. Talent runs in the family because I found out last night she's the artist whose work is all over my back and ass."

My head goes light as the blood drains from it. I cough, then choke on air. Taking advantage of the moment, I move slightly away from Matt. Once I can breathe again, I realize everyone is *still* staring at me. My mouth is so dry I don't bother trying to speak and end up waving like a loon.

Finally, after an excruciating few seconds of silence, Nick Henderson steps forward and holds out his hand. Breaking Giant's drummer is built like a lumberjack and looks like one, too, but his eyes are kind and his smile genuine.

"Nice to meet you, Sophie. I'm Nick. Your brother did most of my ink. He's a master." He waves a pretty redhead forward. "This is my wife, Kat."

I shake both of their hands, feeling marginally more sane. Jackson calls out a greeting from his seat; his date smiles and waves. From the ecstatic expression fixed on her face—and the lack of introduction—I'm guessing she's a newcomer to group functions.

"Hi, Sophie," says Julian Ashburn, reminding me why Breaking Giants is so damn famous—his smokey, deep voice. To my relief, he's smiling now, and so is Rose, who's tucked under his arm.

"Good to see you, Soph," says Rose. "Weekend off?"

"Yeah."

"How's Tullamore?" She pouts. "I miss my baby."

Julian kisses her head. "Don't worry, I'll put one in you soon."

Rose's mouth drops open and she smacks him. Julian just laughs. I laugh, too, feeling ten kinds of awkward. "The café is good. Great. Everything is running smoothly."

God, this is fucking painful.

I point vaguely over my shoulder to Allison and the other normal, not-famous people. "Anyway, it's good to see you, Rose, and great to meet all of you. I'm going to, uh… go that way. Okay, bye."

I don't run toward Allison, but it's a near thing. She gives me a hug, her body shaking like she's trying not to laugh. "Oh, man. That was hard to watch."

I hiss back, "You know I'm not good at peopling."

A laugh breaks free. "You work in the service industry, Soph."

I lean back. "That's different. *They're* different. Basically aliens."

She shrugs. "They're normal once you get to know them. By the way, what the heck was that with Matt? Since when are you guys on a first-name basis?"

I groan. "He came into the café with Josh last night. He also saw my drawing on the wall and figured out that I drew his back piece. Feel free to kill me now."

She laughs harder. "Oh, man. Well, he feels some type of way about it, I'll tell you that much."

I blink. "Huh? What does that mean?"

Katie distracts me by reappearing and handing me a pint glass of dark beer.

"I love you, woman," I say emphatically.

Her smile fades into a wince. "You won't love either of us after we tell you that you have to play on one of their teams." She nods toward the Breaking Giants group.

Beer stalled halfway to my mouth, my gaze bounces between Allison and Katie with increasing horror. "*What?*"

Allison leans close to me, lowering her voice. "I'm really sorry. We had a few people cancel, and I didn't know Jackson was bringing a date. It messed everything up. I tried to split up the teams or make them smaller, even mix up the groups so you could play with Katie and me, but everyone shut me down."

She looks truly miserable, and suddenly, I feel bad. Bowling night is one of her favorite things—she certainly talks about it enough—and my drama is ruining what I know is usually a laid back, fun affair.

"It's okay, Allison. I'm being a brat. Don't worry about me. I'll have fun. This is fun."

She fights a smile at my pitiful attempt at sounding confident. "Thanks, Soph. I seriously owe you. I know how uncomfortable you must feel." She glances over my head, and her eyes gleam when they return to mine. "Incoming."

"Dollface, I hear you're on my team. I've been sent to fetch you."

I send Allison a final dagger glare, then face Matt. Surprisingly, it's getting easier to look at him. Exposure therapy at its finest. He's still the most gorgeous human

I've probably ever seen, but at least my brain is functioning in his presence now.

"I've gotta warn you," I tell him seriously, "I'm horrible at bowling."

He shrugs, pulling a flask from his pocket and taking a deep pull. "So am I." Blue eyes slant to mine before flickering away. "Neither of us wants to be here, so we might as well stick together."

Something in his voice stops me from making a flippant response. I don't know him well enough to understand the undercurrent in his words, but considering the turn his personal life took recently, I feel a pang of sympathy.

"All right," I say on a sigh.

His grin is dazzling as he clanks his flask against my raised glass so hard beer sloshes over my fingers. Feeling like I found a puzzle piece that completes a picture, I realize he's a little drunk.

"Thanks, Dollface."

I grimace. "The nickname has to go, though. How old are you?"

"Ancient at thirty-five," he answers readily, then he waves some fingers toward my head. "Have you seen yourself? That face? The nickname stays. Believe me, if I hadn't sworn off women a few months ago, I'd for sure be trying to take you home. But since sex is off the table, we're going to be friends instead. Great friends. Cool?"

I gape at him and adjust his level of drunkenness from *buzzed* to *hammered*. My face is so hot it's about to melt off. His words ricochet around my stunned brain, not making sense.

This can't be happening.

Matt reads my expression, and whatever he sees wipes the smile off his face. "I shouldn't have said that. About the sex. Sorry." His throat bobs as he swallows; he glances briefly at his bandmates, who thankfully aren't paying attention to us. Then he looks back at me and lowers his voice. "The thing is, I just need a friend right now. And I know it's dumb, but I feel like I already know you after listening to Josh talk about you for years. I'm also a walking poster for your art, in case you forgot, so I feel like in a way, we're already bonded. Like friends."

"I didn't forget," I say weakly, then sigh. "Fine. Friends."

He nods. "And I won't touch you again." At my sharp look, he murmurs, "I felt you flinch when I put my arm around you. I'm sorry."

I swallow so hard my throat cramps, then suck in a breath. "You're forgiven."

His shoulders drop, releasing tension, and he gives

me a smile that I realize is the first *real* one I've seen. It's even more devastating than his others.

"Great. Let's go get shoes and balls." He snorts as he walks—a bit unsteadily—toward the shoe counter where a lone employee watches him approach with adoring eyes. "No touching each other's balls, though. Wait—my balls. Nope. Never mind. Whoa, there's a step here."

I follow a few feet behind him, shaking my head. I don't feel awkward anymore. I feel downright sad.

Matt Sullivan is not okay.

And as insane as it probably is, I'm going to do my best to be his friend tonight.

5

---

*A*llison was right. Bowling is fun, even when you suck, and especially if you don't care about winning. Matt and I get lucky having Jackson and his date—Christina, I found out—as teammates, because they're actually really good.

After the third game of them carrying our sorry assess, Matt and I end up slouched on a couch while the two of them take all four turns. Our current opposing team is headed by Allison, who doesn't mind that we're cheating. I think she's just tickled I stayed longer than an hour.

"My arm hurts," I whine, shifting it away from my body.

"Baby," snorts Matt. "Imagine how my back feels."

Surprisingly, after finishing his flask an hour ago,

Matt stopped drinking. He's still buzzed but no longer saying inappropriate things. To me, at least. I learned fast that he's a heckler. His taunts are so off-the-wall, though, even the recipients laugh.

"Hey, Popeye, I see that arm getting weak! Better find yourself some spinach before you wreck yourself!"

Nick, the target of the comment, ignores it while his wife laughs.

"You're ridiculous," I mutter, taking a sip of ice water. I stopped after my second beer, having no desire to wake up with a headache tomorrow. "They're not even playing us right now."

Matt shrugs, smiling benignly. "No one is spared, Dollface."

Despite my lack of skills making me an easy target, he hasn't heckled me. But I don't point that out.

Shifting with a slight wince that I feel a sympathetic echo of in my own back, Matt faces me on the couch. "I have a question, new best friend."

I keep my eyes on the game, but I know he's looking at me by the distinctive awareness in my body. I'll likely always know—*feel*—when this man looks at me.

"Shoot."

"How come Josh never told me you were the artist of my back piece? He didn't take the credit or anything, but he said you wanted to stay anonymous. Did you really?"

I meet his inquisitive gaze. "Yes. You were his first famous client. I didn't want my art to overshadow his skill. Plus, there's no one else who could have tattooed that design with anywhere near the depth and precision he's capable of."

"I agree," he says easily, then props his arm on the back of the couch. His fingers are less than six inches from my shoulder, which suddenly feels on fire. Looking away, I shift a little to increase the distance between us. He notices; I can feel the change in the air. But he doesn't say anything.

"Why didn't you pursue a career in art?"

This, at least, is an easy one. "You of all people know how hard it is to succeed in a purely creative field when you're not a nepo baby. No matter how good you are, the odds are minuscule."

He nods. "Like being struck by lightning."

I smirk. "Did it hurt?"

"It hurt so good."

He grins wickedly, the same smile that has graced a hundred magazine covers. I'm not immune to the signature, panty-melting expression, but manage not to blush. He can't help it, and I'm not sure he even realizes he's doing it. It's not his fault his parents' DNA created a Nordic god.

"But I get what you're saying," he continues idly.

"Sometimes I think about what would have happened if that talent scout hadn't seen us that night. Would we have slogged along? Barely making ends meet, hustling until we were burned out on music and each other?" He shrugs.

"I tried for a while," I admit, doing my best not to think about my last year in art school. *Stick to the facts.* "I had a few small shows around town, sold a decent amount. But I couldn't keep up with the momentum. You have to commit all of yourself. Your relationships, your sleep, your health... everything takes second place to the art. I couldn't produce fast enough and it wasn't sustainable. I had jobs, bills to pay, and a family that needed my support. I wasn't going to bail on them for some pipe dream..." I trail off and concentrate on my water glass, wishing I'd kept my mouth shut.

After a moment, Matt says softly, "I'm sorry about your dad. And your stepdad. That must have been really hard."

My blood pressure skyrockets as I whip my head up. He holds up both hands. "Josh told me your dad passed away when you guys were little, and that your stepdad bailed. I told you he was a chatty motherfucker." He grimaces. "I have a bad habit of speaking whatever I'm thinking. I'm sorry. I shouldn't have brought it up."

Several deep breaths help. So does a vow to castrate

my big brother. "It's fine. I barely remember my bio dad, honestly. I was five when he died. Josh was almost seven and has a lot more memories." I narrow my gaze. "What else do you know?"

He laughs. "Just general stuff. It's not like he told me your bra size." He winces. "Sorry. Again. Dang, I haven't apologized so much to one person in... probably my life."

I can't help but laugh. "Head to mouth filter really is an issue for you, huh?"

He nods, an adorably contrite expression on his handsome face. "This is new for me." I frown, but he doesn't elaborate. Then his gaze veers past me. "Hey, man, did we win?"

Jackson and Christina approach us, smiling and glued to each other. "Of course," Jackson says smugly, then looks down at Christina with carnal focus. "We're gonna head out."

"Hallelujah! Does that mean we can bail, too?"

"You could have left an hour ago and no one would have noticed."

Matt laughs. "That's cold. Be safe, kids. Don't do anything I wouldn't do."

Jackson rolls his eyes, then looks at me with a warm smile. "It was nice meeting you, Sophie."

"You, too."

Christina smiles and waves as they turn and head for the shoe return. I notice other groups finishing their games, returning shoes, saying goodbyes. Weirdly conflicted—I want to go home, but I don't want the night to end—I unlace my shoes and toe them off.

"So, Dollface, wanna get out of here? I know a great twenty-four-hour breakfast place."

"Uhh..."

"Mike's Diner?" Rose asks from behind me. "We're heading there, too. Sophie, do you want to ride with me and Julian?"

Matt has a weird expression on his face as his gaze slides from Rose to me. I scan the area for Allison, deciding I *do* want this night to be over. I need to get away from these people. There are too many deeply buried emotional landmines.

I pick up my shoes and stand. "Thanks for the offer, but I'm going to head home."

Her smile softens. "At least let us drop you off so you don't have to call an Uber."

Allison and Katie appear like magic, purses over their shoulders. I almost groan with relief. "I've got her, Rose. She doesn't live too far from us."

I send Allison a *thank you* with my eyes, then smile at Rose. "It was great to see you again. Say bye to Julian and the others for me?"

She smiles. "Sure thing."

"I'm gonna return my shoes," I tell Allison. "Meet you outside?"

"Sounds good."

I grab my purse and make a beeline for the counter. After trading niceties—forced on my end—with other players in line, I finally offload the shoes and make a pit stop in the restroom.

Now that I'm on my way home, I can't wait to get there, for this night and all its weird tension to end. I'm suddenly so drained my eyelids feel like lead.

Halfway to the front door, I stop and wince, realizing I didn't say goodbye to Matt.

When I turn around, he's right in front of me.

"Jesus," I gasp, jumping back a step.

"Sorry." He chuckles, then sobers. "Friends don't leave friends without saying goodbye, Dollface."

"I thought you were outside already," I lie.

He shakes his head chidingly and bites his full lower lip, which should be a criminal act for what it does to my body. Then he pulls his phone out of his pocket, unlocks the screen, and hands it to me. "Give me your number."

This is a bad idea. Really bad. The words float on repeat in my head, dizzyingly fast, as I input my contact info, then hand the phone back to him. Our fingers connect; warmth zings from my breasts to my belly.

Bad, bad idea.

Matt's lips quirk. "Thanks."

"You're welcome."

Sliding his hands into the pockets of his jeans, he says nothing. Just stares at me. We're standing in a darker area. I can't read his eyes.

I clear my throat. "Well, have a good night."

"You, too."

"I'm leaving now," I say with a hint of exasperation.

"Cool. I'm waiting for you to walk away."

I shake my head, fighting a smile. "You're a weird one, Matt Sullivan."

"You have no idea." The words are gravelly and deep, thick with innuendo.

"What—" I stop myself and lift a hand. "Never mind, I don't want to know."

His gaze flickers down my body before narrowing on my face. "It's really too bad we're just friends."

A laugh burbles in my throat. "Stop, seriously. Turn it off."

"I can't *turn it off*, Dollface. This is my normal state."

For whatever reason, the words dim my smile. "I don't think that's true."

His own smile melts away. "You'd be the first." Then

comes a self-deprecating chuckle, the mask sliding back into place. He holds out his fist between us. When I stare at it, his brows lift. "Since we aren't hugging friends, we're going to fist bump."

Lips twitching, I tap my fist to his.

"Soph? You coming?" calls Katie from the front door.

"Yep! Bye, Matt."

"So long, Sophie."

I hurry toward Katie. As the door closes behind me, I glance back. True to his word, he watched me walk away.

6

week goes by and my phone stays silent beyond the usual mix of calls from family, friends, and scam bots asking me about my auto warranty.

Some mornings, I wake up and don't immediately remember the strangeness of last weekend, but more often than not, I do. I go to sleep and wake up thinking about it—about *him*—replaying every word, every almost touch. I try to read between lines that aren't clear to begin with. His shameless flirting and flippant, irreverent attitude. The rare moments of vulnerability and sensitivity.

"I felt you flinch when I touched you."

"I'm sorry about your dad."

"You'd be the first."

The last words, and the way he said them, bother me the most—the implication that everyone expects him to act a certain way, that he's been locked into the same role for so long no one believes he can change. So he doesn't bother trying.

Is that what ended his engagement? Did his fiancée lose trust in him because he didn't stop flirting with other women? Did he *cheat* on her? As repugnant as the thought is, I find it hard to imagine. I honestly can't see Matt being in a committed relationship and disrespecting his partner that way.

Which I recognize is naïve as hell.

I don't know Matt Sullivan beyond our interactions last weekend and his long-standing, public reputation as a connoisseur of hedonism. Six years ago, I saw blatant evidence of it, and I've never read a conflicting opinion online. The man loves women, his band, and partying nonstop. I definitely wasn't the only one who was shocked when he got engaged.

At the end of the day, I don't—might never—know what happened with his ex. Just because I've harbored a minor obsession with him for close to a decade doesn't mean he's not exactly what his reputation paints him as: a shameless womanizer.

"If I hadn't sworn off women a few months ago, I'd for sure be trying to take you home."

"It's really too bad we're just friends."

But we aren't friends. I honestly doubt we ever can be. Even if the flirting was just habit for him, and he didn't mean a word he said, I can't turn off my attraction to him any more than he can turn off his stupidly perfect face.

"Sophie?"

I look away from my computer screen to find Dania leaning in the doorway of my office. "What's up?"

"Greta and the baby are here in case you want to say hi."

"Awesome timing," I say, smiling. Owen's toddler is ridiculously cute, and his wife, Greta, is a sweetheart. "I need a break from doing inventory."

Dania laughs; we all know how annoying inventory is. "You're welcome. Random question: does Owen have a sister? There's a woman with Greta who looks just like him."

I know instantly who it is—Rose. Only I'm not sure I want to see her. Not after all the weird vibes last weekend.

"Rose Cunningham," I tell Dania, who looks at me blankly. "You seriously don't know who Rose Cunningham is?"

A few years ago, Rose's songs all but hijacked the radio, and she opened for Breaking Giants on their last worldwide tour. Her sophomore album went gold, though I haven't heard anything about her releasing another or touring again soon. She's a local legend in her own right and doubly famous since she married Julian.

Dania's eyes widen in realization. "Ohh, *Rose!* As in the former co-owner, Owen's cousin?"

"I'm surrounded by children," I groan, shaking my head in mock disappointment. Dania is eighteen and listens to whatever her generation is into, which changes seemingly weekly and hops genres faster than I can keep up.

"What?" asks my clueless employee.

"Never mind, just feeling my age. I'm almost done with inventory. Be out in a bit."

When she's gone, I lean back in my chair and stare out the nearby window for a few minutes. My stomach growls, reminding me I skipped lunch. As I'm debating whether or not I can sneak into the kitchen without being seen, there's a knock on my half-closed door.

"Yeah?"

"Sophie? It's Rose. Can I come in?"

Shit.

"Sure."

She walks in and drops into the chair opposite the desk. Curly dark hair haloes her head. Sunlight through the window makes her hazel eyes glow warmly, matching the smile she gives me.

"How are you?" she asks.

"Great, thanks. You?"

"Really good." She leans forward, then back, and finally crosses her arms over her chest. "So, uh, this is pretty awkward, but there's actually something I wanted to talk to you about."

I decide against playing dumb. Rose has always been nice to me, and I can tell she's as uncomfortable as I am.

"You want to talk about Matt."

She relaxes, a smile tilting her lips. "Yeah. Julian told me to leave it alone, but I couldn't. I feel... protective of him, I guess. He's fragile right now and I don't want to see him get hurt again."

Say what?

I blink in stupefaction. "I'm totally lost."

Rose sighs, her gaze darting around the office before snapping to me. "I shouldn't even be telling you this, but I'm going with my gut, which tells me you're someone I can trust. Melody did a number on Matt. Not at first, obviously. She was good for him. Really good. He grew up a lot. Matured. They were happy, I think."

She frowns, eyes unfocused. I get the sense she's half-forgotten I'm in the room. "Actually, I don't know anymore. If they were happy, I mean. Melody didn't get along with his family—I still don't know why and neither of them would talk about it. I know they argued a fair amount. Melody and I used to be close, but that changed. Same with Matt. He used to be an open book, but now... None of us even know exactly what happened. Melody just packed up and moved to Chicago three months ago. She left me a voicemail saying the wedding was off." She sighs again, refocusing on me. "Sorry. I know this is a lot."

Feeling totally off-kilter, I manage, "Why are you telling me all this?"

"Maybe I feel protective of you, too," she says softly, studying me with an intensity that makes me itch. "I'm immune to Matt's charisma, but that doesn't mean I don't know its power. Don't be his rebound, Sophie. In the state he's in right now, he'll leave you in pieces."

I sag back into my chair, my heart thumping hard. Confusion and annoyance war for dominance in my head. Finally, I peel my tongue off the roof of my mouth.

"I appreciate the concern, Rose," I say, and even I can hear the thread of affront in it. I take a breath and try again, managing a softer tone. "But it's not like that with Matt and me. I have no desire whatsoever to date him. And sorry for being blunt, but what you said doesn't make a lot of sense. You told me you want to protect him from being hurt again, then said he'll leave me in pieces."

She winces. "You're right, it makes no sense. Probably why Julian told me to keep my mouth shut. I just had a feeling, I guess. Maybe it was seeing you two together on Saturday. The way he looked at you, like you could solve all his problems."

If I didn't have a bunch of nosy friends and an even nosier family, I'd probably be more angry at Rose right now. She's definitely crossing a line, but I can sense her genuine concern and confusion. She's trying to help. To protect someone she loves.

"I haven't spoken to him since Saturday," I tell her. "He asked for my number but hasn't called."

She nods, looking distracted. "They've been in the studio a lot this week. He'll call you, though. I know him."

Nerves trill, but I ignore them. "Regardless of what you think you saw on Saturday, Matt and I agreed—several times—that we would be just friends. I'm not interested in dating anyone, let alone being someone's rebound." I sigh. "What do you want me to say, Rose? That I won't answer the phone if he calls?"

Surprising me, she laughs. "You should tell me to fuck off and stop meddling."

A smile pulls at my mouth. "I didn't want to be rude. But I was thinking it."

She makes a sound between a laugh and a groan, then drops her head into her hands. "*God.* I'm all over the place right now. My mood swings have mood swings." She looks up, eyes bright and slightly panicked, then whispers, "I might be pregnant. I'm late but haven't taken a test. I'm in denial, I think."

I look toward the door, hoping against hope that someone will come save me. It stays empty. "Uhh, congratulations?"

She laughs again, high and shrill, then stands abruptly. "I'm sorry, Sophie. I shouldn't have come back here. I've made a big mess and I don't know how to clean it up." Her eyes well with tears. "I love Matt like a brother. I guess that's my only defense. I'm sorry if it felt like I was attacking you."

Alarmed, I stand up and round the desk. "It's okay, Rose. Really. I have siblings, so I get it. When Josh's ex-girlfriend broke his heart, I entered her address on a bunch of Jehovah's Witness websites requesting visits to her house."

Rose slaps a hand to her mouth, eyes wide with hilarity.

"Oh, and when a boy asked my kid sister on her first date, Josh and I cornered him after school and interviewed him for an hour. He dumped her the next day. She wouldn't speak to us for months. We do crazy shit for people we love."

Rose dissolves into laughter. "Thanks for being cool about this. I can see why Matt..." She shakes her head. "You now what? I'm learning from my mistakes and keeping my mouth shut."

"Ha, probably a good idea."

She turns to leave, then pauses in the door, her hazel eyes soft on mine. "Take care of yourself. I'm pretty sure I'll see you soon."

As soon as she's gone, I close the door and collapse into my chair, wondering what the fuck just happened.

The buzz of a text message comes from my purse on the floor by my feet. My heart jackknifes before I can tell it to calm down. There's no way it's Matt. That would be beyond weird timing.

Sure, we had fun hanging out on Saturday, but what does that mean? Nothing. He's a friendly, chatty dude. It's no wonder he and my brother get along.

When there's another buzz from my purse, I grab my phone. Multiple texts in a row usually mean my mother, who has the bad habit of using text-to-speech and accidentally hitting send mid-sentence.

But it's not my mother.

Hey, Dollface. Did you miss me?

What are you doing Tuesday night?
There's a band playing Lotus Lounge
that I wanna check out. You down?

I've been thinking about what my best
friend said about how hard it is to make
it in this industry

I'd like to start showing up more in the
local scene. Giving my support and
whatnot

But I need a wingman. Wing-woman?
My boys are all boring and
whipped now

My fingers hover over the text box. I tap the heel of my other hand repeatedly to my forehead, hoping to jog loose some common sense. Or better yet, a sense of self-preservation, because I'm suddenly sure that Rose was right. He'll break me.

Matt Sullivan is like the storm on his back. And I'm the boat.

I type out a reply, then delete it, aggravated that I'm off Tuesday and lying doesn't come more easily to me.

I can see dots. Stop arguing with
yourself and say yes

Fine. I'm in

Smart choice. I'm a lot of fun and you need more fun in your life

I'll pick you up. where do you live?

I'll meet you there. It's a five minute walk from my apartment

Deal

See you at 8 on Tuesday, bestie

I bite my traitorous lips, which want to stretch in a grin.

you're ridiculous

you love it

see you tuesday

don't forget

or I'll find a new bff

I close out my messages and drop my phone on the desk, then stare at my shaking fingers.

What did I just do?

7

Sunday and Monday drag like molasses, but Tuesday flies by. I almost cancel a thousand times, especially when my mom invites me over for dinner. I hate telling her no, even though she's over the moon with happiness when I mention I have plans with a friend.

I've never had much of a social life, but in the last year, I've become kind of a recluse. I see Kelly a few times a month but rarely join in group outings. I know my mom worries about me, probably more than her other kids because of what happened during my last year of college. But despite my career choice, I've always been more of an introvert than the rest of my siblings.

Give me a sketchpad, a cup of coffee, and my couch, and I'm happy.

"It's not a date," I tell my three-year-old tabby, Pickle, who's been watching me mess with my hair for ten minutes. Eventually, I give up and leave it loose but pull a rubber band onto my wrist just in case.

Pickle meows from the bed.

"What's that, buddy? You don't feel good? Should I stay home?"

He blinks imperiously at me just as my phone buzzes.

> you're late

> i have your ticket

> get your fine ass over here

I sigh, wincing when I glance back in the mirror and see my flushed cheeks.

> on my way

The walk does nothing to alleviate my steadily climbing nerves, despite the temperate air and the beautiful golden hour light of the summer evening.

By the time Lotus Lounge comes into view, I feel like I've been sprinting. There's a crowd outside, which is weird for Tuesday—until I spot a blond head smack in the middle of it, a few inches above everyone else.

Matt's height means he sees me a second after I see him. "Excuse me, everyone," he says, moving toward me, brushing people away like they're flies in his orbit. The closer he gets, the more I notice the pinched skin around his eyes. He stops right in front of me, so close I have to crane my neck.

I have the fleeting thought that maybe he was going to hug me before he stopped himself.

"You okay?" I ask, shifting back a step.

Surprise flares in his eyes before he nods. "Yeah. Comes with the territory." He glances over his shoulder, where a good number of people are still staring at him and whispering. "Let's go inside. I'll buy you a root beer."

I laugh as we head for the doors. "A root beer? What am I, five?"

His glance sears me. "No way you're drinking tonight. Too many creeps around, and you get flirty when you drink."

I sputter. "What? First of all, controlling much? And second, how would you even know that?"

He smirks as he hands our tickets to the bouncer at the door, ignoring the awe on the guy's face. "You were drinking Saturday. You were flirty. In fact, I think from now on you should only drink if I'm around. By the way, you look like a cat burglar in all black. I like it. And I really like those pants. They're, uh... nice."

I bite my cheek on a laugh. "What is wrong with you?"

He shrugs, throwing me an unrepentant grin. "I'm challenging myself to compliment you without making it pervy."

For better or worse, there's a decent turnout for the acts tonight, and we don't talk as we make our way to the bar. Matt walks first, forging a path effortlessly with his height and larger-than-life presence. He even glances back every few feet to make sure I'm still with him. It makes me feel special and also like a giant fraud.

There are beautiful women all around us, eyeing him with hunger and me with sharp looks that say, "I should be in your shoes." They probably should. But the stares also make me want to grab the fingers that flex periodically at Matt's side. A long-buried part of my psyche spits out dirt and tries to convince me it's because he wants to reach back and grab my hand.

But he doesn't. Obviously. Because we're *friends*. And even my friends don't usually touch me, a fact he picked up on with remarkable speed and seems intent on respecting.

When Matt reaches the counter, he lifts his arm and waves me beneath it. I hesitate for a second, but then someone shoulder-checks me. My skin crawls and I duck past Matt until I'm flush with the bar. His arms come down on either side of me, not touching, but effectively blocking me from everyone around us. His body radiates heat onto my spine, and I don't think I've ever been more aware of the space that separates my body from another's.

"Thanks," I say, hazarding a glance back at him.

His gaze drops over my face, settling for a taut second on my mouth. "I protect my friends," he says with a little smile, then looks at the bartender, who has magically appeared in front of us—even though a dozen people were here first.

Matt orders a Whiskey Sour. His head lowers, breath warming the hair over my ear. "What do you want?"

I shiver as the vibrations of his voice roll through me. "Root beer, duh."

He chuckles. "I was just messing with you."

I shrug. "I'm feeling root beer, honestly."

He relays my request, and we wait for our drinks. Both the crowd and the noise level steadily increase around us. A few people jostle his back. His arms flex to prevent our bodies from touching, but it's a losing battle.

When I hear him curse under his breath, I turn sideways, my shoulder falling firmly against his chest. Ignoring the fizzy warmth that cascades through me at the feel of his hard chest, I look up at him. He stills, one brow lifted and his eyes narrowed.

"I'm not going to freak out if you touch me, Matt," I say clearly. "I don't like strangers touching me. You're not a stranger."

A slow smile curves his lips. "I'm your best friend."

I chuckle. "Whatever."

He looks like he's going to say something else, but our drinks are placed on the counter. He drops a twenty-dollar bill and we start navigating back through the crowd. This time it's harder to stay close to him.

This time, instead of his hand flexing at his side, it stretches back toward me. I don't think as I grab it, as his fingers curl around mine and squeeze.

THE OPENING ACTS ARE DECENT, but the headliner, a trio whose sound reminds me of a mix between the National and Night Riots, is good. Really good.

Halfway through their second song—which has a driving beat that's making the crowd surge—a man taps Matt's shoulder and yells something at him. Matt nods in response, then leans down, lips grazing my ear as he says, "Ready for some perks of having me as your bestie?"

My reply gets taken, along with the air in my lugs, as someone slams into my back. Matt catches me against his chest, an arm curling around my lower back to steady me.

I suddenly can't breathe, but not from panic. I can feel every single inch of me touching every inch of him. My hands on his muscular shoulders, my breasts against his chest, my mouth millimeters from the bare, tattooed skin in the V of his T-Shirt, his belt pressing into my abdomen, his...

I jerk back, gasping, "Sorry."

He swallows and shakes his head. "Come on." Taking my hand, he pulls me toward a door beside the stage, where the guy who talked to him waits.

Seconds later, we're in the relative privacy of the wings, with a perfect view of the band and hidden from the crowd. Matt even drags a couple of chairs over so we can sit.

"Better, yeah?" he asks with a teasing grin.

I nod and summon a smile, but I'm still reeling inside.

A minute passes.

"Hey, Dollface, you good?"

I meet his concerned eyes. "Yep."

He doesn't look like he believes me, but thankfully he doesn't press the issue.

I can't stand the awkwardness for long. Between songs, I lean toward him. "They're pretty good, right? I mean, I don't have your refined musical ear or anything, but still."

His broad smile tugs an answering one from me. "Yes. They're damn good. Wanna stay a bit after with me? I want to introduce myself, check out their tour schedule, maybe wrangle a scout from my label to come see them."

I grin back. "Definitely."

8

This woman.

This freaking woman.

Sophie Marshall.

I'm still half-hard when I get home to my giant, dark house. For the first time in the last three months, I don't even notice the yawning absence. My head is sideways over my new *friend*.

I can still smell her shampoo from having her thick, soft hair floating under my nose most of the night. And her skin—no artificial perfume to be found, just *her*. Natural, with a faint hint of a lotion she used recently.

I walk into the kitchen and pour a glass of water, rubbing my chest absently as I remember her soft, full breasts pressed against me. I swear I felt her nipples harden before she jerked away, her eyes wide with shock—and desire.

I saw it. I know I did.

Not that I'm going to do anything about it.

"Fuck," I growl.

The tattoos and those full lips. The dark green eyes. The long, tawny hair. Those tight fucking pants. Her juicy ass and flaring hips. She's a fantasy with legs for days and a smile that makes me think there's hope for the world.

Her shyness and the way it's slowly fading around me? The way she looks at me sometimes like I'm a cross between a loaded weapon and a tree she wants to climb? It all just makes me more curious about her. About her private life. Private thoughts. Ambitions and fears and dreams.

I think about her art on my back, stretching from my shoulders to across my glutes, which only makes me think about her hands on my skin. About the sounds she makes when she comes. Does she sigh and whimper, or does she scream?

My cock instantly swells, and I'm disgusted with myself. Disgusted because it means Melody was right. She threw a lot of verbal shit at me during our last fight, but her final tirade really took the cake.

"I'm not enough for you, Matt. And frankly, you're not enough for me. We want different things. I'm going to Chicago for my PhD and you're going to find another woman in no time. You won't even miss me. Not really."

Pain flares deep in my chest where my heart used to be. At the time, I believed she was wrong. I still sometimes do. Then I remember what she said next.

"Let's be real. The only reason you asked me to marry you is because Julian and Nick found their forever people and you felt left behind just like you did as a kid. It was never about me. About us. It was always about what others thought of you."

Slamming my hand against the faucet to turn the water back on, I duck my face into the stream, letting it run over my face and into my hair.

"You won't even miss me."

I do miss her. But I'm not sure anymore if what I miss is her or the idea of her, of having a partner. A wife and a family. Kids who will run around with my bandmates' brats at a backyard barbecue someday.

I honestly don't know what I was thinking getting involved with someone who had a master's in Psychology. From the get-go, Melody psychoanalyzed literally everyone in our life. She judged Julian for his commitment to Alcoholics Anonymous, which she saw as inferior to psychotherapy. She judged Rose for not prioritizing her music career, unwilling to accept that she might actually know her own mind.

I never questioned who I was, why I was the way I was, until I met Melody. And mostly, I think being with her made me a better person. A better man.

As frustrating and painful as a lot of it was, she forced me to look at the world in a new way. To consider the impact I have on others, the gravity and consequence of my actions both small and large.

And then she broke my fucking heart.

Dropping my wallet and keys on the kitchen island, I trudge upstairs, not bothering to turn on any lights. In the bathroom, I turn on the shower and strip. My skin feels raw. Pressurized. My lower back itches where it's still healing from the needle.

I step under the shower head and close my eyes, dropping my forehead to the cool tile.

Green eyes float in my mind. Dark lashes. Blushing cheeks. Nipples that will be the same dark rose as her lips. Tattoos hidden beneath her clothes that I want to map with my tongue.

Groaning, I thump my head against the wall, refusing to relieve the insane pressure in my balls. Refusing to believe Melody was right about me finding another woman *in no time.*

But even more than that, I can't handle the thought that she was right about the other thing—that she wasn't enough for me or me for her.

Because the way Sophie has me twisted makes me think it's true. I've known her for a week. Been in her presence longer than five minutes a grand total of twice.

And I want her more than I've wanted anything.

Anyone.

Ever.

9

August's heat shifts to September's warmth, which lingers throughout the month, though not without the promise of impending cold in the mornings and evenings. Soon, the leaves will start to change and my favorite season will officially begin.

As the world's axis shifts over the course of six weeks, I don't hear from Matt. Even though it sometimes feels like a physical compulsion, I don't text him. There's no reason to. He has his life and I have mine. For all his teasing about our status as best friends, we aren't. He isn't anything to me.

If only I believed that.

I sketch his face a hundred times, from a hundred angles, throwing away every page until the cover of my sketchbook lists sadly. Then I throw the whole thing out and buy a new one, vowing not to draw him.

My abstinence lasts two days.

The second-to-last weekend in September is my weekend off. I spend most of it with Mom and Beka. Josh is booked solid both days, and Patrick is too cool for our movie marathons now. At least he broke up with Bronx at the beginning of the month. Apparently, her ex-husband wasn't her *ex* at all, and he's up for parole in December.

My little brother might be smarter than he looks.

When I get home early evening on Sunday after finishing the last Harry Potter movie and too much Pad Thai, I collapse onto my couch and pull a blanket over me. Like clockwork, twenty seconds later, Pickle pounces on my chest and commences making biscuits on my boobs—hence the blanket.

My phone buzzes in my back pocket. I pull it out with a yawn, wondering if I forgot something at Mom's.

Then I see his name, and my stomach does a backflip.

> I think our label is gonna sign that band we saw. cool huh?

The first wave of emotion to sweep through me is

annoyance, while the second, bigger wave is a muddy mix of elation, longing, and nervousness.

He texted me.

I wish I had control over the adrenaline crackling through my limbs. My suddenly choppy breath. I hate the effect he has on me, almost enough to not reply. But I'm not that disciplined.

> friends don't ignore friends for six weeks

> that's weird. I don't see any texts or missed calls from you

I wince. He's right. But I'm still annoyed.

> whatever, Matt

The three dots appear, disappear, then reappear.

> I'm sorry

> wanna hang tomorrow? we'll be in the studio most of the day, but you're welcome to come.

> Rose will be there

I frown at the phone. *Is he serious?* While the idea of listening to Breaking Giants record music would have made me faint with excitement a few months ago, now I can't imagine anything I'd rather do less.

Not after Rose's visit to Tullamore. And definitely not after the last month and a half of silence from Matt.

Thankfully, I have an easy excuse.

I'm working

Tuesday?

No. Working

What about right now? I'll come over

Matt…

There's a long pause.

Okay, Dollface. I'm a big boy and can take a hint.

Have a good night

I toss my phone onto the couch, almost hitting Pickle, who stares at me like I shit in his food.

Then another wave of emotion hits me, the biggest one of all: regret.

"What do I do?" I ask Pickle.

He licks his chops.

Cursing my weakness, I pick up my phone and text a rockstar my address.

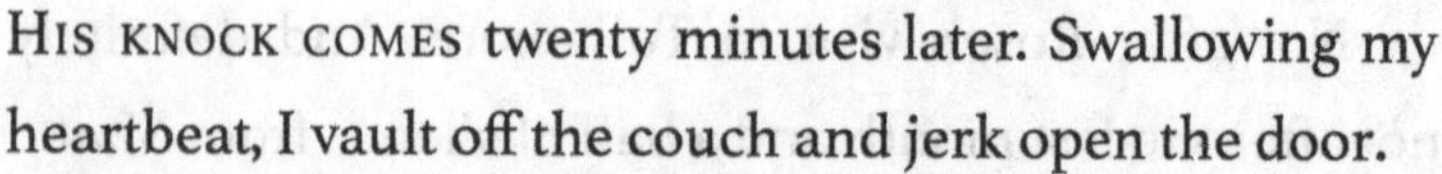

His knock comes twenty minutes later. Swallowing my heartbeat, I vault off the couch and jerk open the door.

His brows lift. "You should ask who it is before opening the door. It could have been a stranger."

He's right, of course. Normally, I would have pepper spray in my hand, too. My brain is clearly on the fritz.

"Hello to you, too," I say, hoping he doesn't notice how my hand trembles when I wave him into my apartment. He walks in, sucking the air out of my small place with every rise of his chest.

I follow him into my cramped living room slash kitchen, clasping my arms by the elbows as he looks around my private space. The mismatched furniture. The art—some framed, some not—all over the walls. The shoes by the door, the overflowing laundry basket in the short hallway leading to my bedroom and bathroom. Dirty dishes in my sink, coffee rings on the countertop, tiny kitchen table overrun with sketchbooks and cases of my favorite art pencils...

Why didn't I spend the twenty minutes cleaning?

I'm strung so tight, I almost tell him this is a mistake and ask him to leave.

"I like it," he says abruptly, turning to me with a grin. "It's very you."

I snort. "You think I'm chaotic?"

He shakes his head chidingly and lifts a paper grocery bag. "I brought ice cream. I didn't know what you liked, so I got a few flavors."

"What if I'm lactose intolerant?"

Matt fixes his beautiful eyes on my face, his lips curved in a half-smile. "You're going to make this hard for me. I can respect that. Will it help if I say I almost texted you every day?"

My heart races. "Why didn't you?"

His gaze flies over my face. Butterfly-wing sensation follows. "Would you accept 'it's complicated' as an answer?"

I swallow, then nod. "Yeah. For now."

His smile widens as he heads for the kitchen and deposits three pints of ice cream in my freezer, then opens my fridge and peers inside. He moves like he's perfectly comfortable, like he naturally dominates every space he occupies. It's unnerving, though not surprising. He probably owns the air in his dentist's office and the DMV, too.

"What are you looking for?" I ask, moving toward him.

"I'm just being nosy," he answers easily, then reaches back into the grocery bag, lifting out a six-pack of glass beer bottles. He removes two from the cardboard and pops the rest in the fridge. "Bottle opener?"

"Drawer to your left."

He finds it, opens the beers, and brings one to me.

"Thanks," I say weakly.

He bites his lip, eyes laughing at me. "You're nervous."

I roll my eyes. "Don't take it personally. There hasn't been a man in my apartment in close to a year."

As soon as the words are out, I blanch. *Fucking idiot.*

I'm surprised, though, when Matt's expression softens, and he nods to himself like I answered a question that wasn't asked.

Walking past me, he drops onto my couch and throws his legs on my coffee table. Then he almost throws his beer as Pickle jumps on his lap and starts kneading his thighs.

"Where the fuck did the cat come from?" he asks, laughing as he looks up at me.

"He's a professional ninja."

Matt strokes a hand over Pickle's back. Pickle freezes and looks back at him. After a few tense moments of man and cat staring at each other, judgment is rendered. Pickle returns to kneading Matt's jeans, his broken-motor purr rumbling in our ears.

Something in my chest melts. Taking a sharp

breath, I skirt around the coffee table and sit in the opposite corner of the couch, pulling a blanket over my legs.

"Is this a sign that we're meant to be friends?" asks Matt, teasing eyes flickering to me. "Tell me this cat hates everyone."

I laugh. "Sorry, buddy. He'd make biscuits on a burglar."

"Damn." He shifts back suddenly. "Whoa, dude, a little close to the family jewels there."

I click my tongue. Pickle stands up, stretches, and saunters over to my lap, where he curls up in a fuzzy brown ball. Matt stares at the cat, blinks, then looks away. I must hallucinate, because for a second... it looked like he was jealous of Pickle.

I grab the TV remote from the arm of the couch. "Movie?" I ask, too loudly.

"Yes, please. I'll watch anything."

I pull up my Netflix account. "*Texas Chainsaw Massacre* or *The Hills Have Eyes*?"

I grin as Matt's eyes widen comically. "Dollface! I would have *never* taken you for a horror fan. I was fully prepared to watch some ridiculously long, boring art noir film."

I laugh. "Josh and I got into horror when we were teens. It's like a cuddly blanket at this point."

He eyes my lap. "Speaking of cuddly blankets, where's mine?"

Leaning forward, I grab another blanket from the back of the couch and toss it at him. He pulls it up to his nose, then tucks it under his chin and snuggles back into the couch, one arm free for his beer.

"Did you just sniff my blanket?" I ask on a horrified laugh. *Oh God, does it stink?*

"Yep," he says, flashing me a crooked grin. "Smells good. Like you."

Blood surges to my cheeks. I look away with a stilted laugh. "So, uh, which movie?"

"I don't care, but I want to talk first."

"Talk?" I squeak. Pickle chirrups, annoyed by my sudden stiffness. I force myself to relax. "About what?"

Matt rolls his head toward me. "Tell me what you've been up to since I saw you last."

"Nothing. I mean, the usual. Work. Hanging with my family." *Drawing your face.*

He takes a sip of beer, and I do the same. It's tasty. A fancy IPA I'd never buy for myself because of the price tag.

"Dating?" he asks casually.

I swallow my mouthful of beer before I spit it out. "No." And because I have no control over my mouth, I ask, "You?"

He shakes his head. "I'm on a hiatus from women for another six months. Rose and I have a wager going that I can't stay single for a year. I'm gonna win."

"That's, uh… weird, honestly."

He laughs, but there's a thread of bitterness to it. "She told me she ambushed you at Tullamore and dumped all my baggage on you." He pauses. "That's part of why I didn't reach out."

"She didn't really—" I stop myself. "No, you're right. She totally ambushed me. I'm sorry. I feel like I should have told you."

He shrugs. "It's only fair, since I know a bunch of random shit about you from Josh. He never told me about the horror film thing, though. I feel cheated."

I force a laugh. "Now I have to know everything he told you, so I can decide whether or not to break his kneecaps."

He chuckles. "Nothing crazy. He told me you were a wicked good artist, and he said you guys were like second parents to your younger siblings growing up. He mentioned your little sister's heart issues." His eyes slide to me. "How's she doing?"

"Good," I answer with a smile. "She gets regular checkups, plus stress tests and stuff like that. But she lives a normal life for the most part. She's an annoying teenager."

"I have a little sister, too—Erin—so I know what you mean. Growing up, she followed me around like a freaking shadow." He's smiling, a soft look in his eyes. "She's thirty now. Still annoying, obviously."

I laugh. "Is she local?"

He nods. "She's a vet. Lives and works in Bellingham."

"The rest of your family around, too?"

"My mom and stepdad, yeah." A shadow passes through his eyes. "My dad split when I was eleven. Decided he wanted a new family with his secretary. Didn't hear a peep from him until I hit it big—now he sends me cards on every holiday like I give a shit. Like he wants credit for making me who I am."

He takes a heavy swallow of beer. "Once a year, usually around Father's Day, he calls me and asks for money. When I was younger and dumber, I made the mistake of giving him some. I thought it would shut him up, get him out of my life, but it just made him worse."

My face screws up in disgust. "That sucks. I'm sorry."

He shrugs. "We all have our shit."

I shift on the couch. Pickle takes offense and hops off my lap, meeping as he wanders toward his water bowl. "And your stepdad? Do you guys get along?"

Matt smiles. "Yeah, Bill's good people. I can't tell you how many times I've tried to buy him and Mom a bigger house, but the most he's let me do is pay off their mortgage."

I laugh lightly to cover a twinge of unease. With the amount of money Matt has, he might as well live on a different planet than me. My monthly budget is my bible. I hope to start saving for a down payment on a small house someday, but student loans and credit card payments suck up most of my overflow cash each month.

The pennies that are left, I usually funnel to my mom. She has a full-time office job now, with a decent wage, but Patrick and Beka are still at home. Between ongoing medical expenses and the fact Patrick eats his weight in food each week, she still needs all the help she can get.

I know she hates it when I sneak bills into her wallet. Even Josh has told me to stop—he makes a good living and is much more equipped to help her, which he does—but I do it, anyway.

"I made you uncomfortable," murmurs Matt. "Was it the money shit?"

I shrug a shoulder, feeling on edge. Frankly, I'm wondering what he's doing here. What *we're* doing.

"Why are you really here, Matt?"

I'm more surprised by my blurted question than him. He sets his beer on the coffee table and sits up, turning to face me with an arm over the back of the couch. His gaze is direct, the blue so disarming I can barely maintain eye contact.

"Honestly? I don't know. Why'd you invite me?"

"Honestly?" I echo. "I don't know, either."

I do know. I know exactly why. Because he's the suck of a mighty wave and I'm flotsam on the water.

"Maybe you should go," I whisper.

"Dollface," he murmurs. "I don't want to go."

My pulse speeds. "Whatever you want from me, I can't give you."

A brow lifts. "What is it you think I want?"

I pinch the bridge of my nose. At my wit's end, I snap, "I have no idea. Sex, possibly? Which isn't going to happen."

"Why not?" he asks, but not arrogantly. He sounds genuinely curious. A touch concerned. He's trying to connect the dots of my aversion to touch and come up with a reason why, like he actually cares.

"Childhood trauma compounded by adult trauma," I say shortly. "And before you feel sorry for me, I'm not celibate. I've had plenty of partners over the years. But this"—I wave a hand between us—"I don't do."

"Intimacy," he says softly, like it's a revelation.

I nod. "So if you're trying to get in my pants, maybe stop trying to get to know me."

Matt chews on his lips, an adorable furrow on his forehead. "You're literally the first woman to say something like that to me," he muses, almost to himself. "Most women want to have sex with me because they're hoping I'll fall in love with them."

I wince. "That's sad."

A grin passes over his face like sunlight through clouds. "I definitely didn't think so in my twenties. But yeah, it got old." He clears his throat. "So, if the issue is that we're attracted to each other—"

"I never said that."

His pointed glance is so droll I almost smile. "Give me a break. You're blushing right now. You should stop, by the way. It just makes me think about where else you're turning red."

I groan and palm my heated face. "Matt—"

"As I was saying," he continues on a cough. "The issue is that we can't sleep together because one, I'm off women at the moment—and I have a bet I'm going to win—and two, you don't do emotional intimacy with your sex partners." I can hear his grin as he adds, "Which means you already like me too much. Does that about sum it up?"

I squirm on the couch, pressing my back against the arm and wishing I could melt into it. "I guess," I mutter. "Although the 'like' part is debatable."

He just laughs. "Liar. Anyway, I have a new proposal. An experiment, if you will."

I peek at him over my fingers. "What?"

"We go on friend dates once a week. No touching. No flirting—except you have to allow me one comment every time we see each other. I'm just not going to be able to help myself."

I stare at the ceiling. "This is so bizarre."

Matt leans forward, eyes alight with boyish excitement. "I'm not done. It gets better. Listen. Friend dates once a week. When six months are up, we reconvene and decide whether we want to continue being friends, or if we want to try something else."

"Something else?" I whisper.

"Yup." He glances at my mouth. "Something else."

10

"I can't even handle this," Kelly whisper-hisses when I finish telling her about last night. Her eyes show whites around the edges. I think she's only blinked once or twice in the last ten minutes.

I don't know how it happened—temporary insanity is the most likely culprit—but I ended up agreeing to Matt's absurd experiment. We even shook on it before I kicked him out of my apartment. I kept his beer and ice cream and watched a movie by myself. A movie I couldn't pay attention to because my body felt like it was sustaining prolonged electroshock.

Lukewarm coffee sits untouched in front of me while Kelly nibbles on a danish. She's done working for the day and I'm on my evening meal break. The café is mostly empty, the music mellow, reflecting the mood of the whole city as it sighs beneath the first rain of the season.

The storm moved in last night. I'm not usually prone to fanciful thinking, but it seems oddly symbolic.

"I don't even know what to say," she mumbles. "I mean, did you tell him why you... you know?"

"Of course not," I say quickly. "I barely know him, Kelly. It took me over a year to even tell you, and I've known you since we were kids."

"True." She chews, nodding thoughtfully. "Completely unrelated—do you even realize you signed up for six months of celibacy?"

"Whoa, no. That's his deal, not mine. We never talked about me not having sex. It doesn't even make sense. We're friends. Friends don't control other friends' sex lives."

She looks at me like I'm daft. "You think he's going to be cool with you sleeping with other dudes?"

"He doesn't have a say. Not my fault he made a bet with Rose." There's an immediate pinch in my conscience, and a louder voice in my head telling me I'm not going to bring home a random dude just to scratch an itch. Not while I have a trashcan full of crumpled sketches of Matt freaking Sullivan, and the real-life man taking up space in my life.

"You don't mean that," observes my best friend, one eye squinting at me.

I sigh. "I don't. But I wish I did."

Kelly gives up on her danish and reaches across the table to cradle my free hand between both of hers. She's one of the few people whose touch never triggers me.

"This is complicated as fuck. Hot, but a total mess. He's obviously into you, Sophie. This whole experiment thing is just a way for him to keep you in his orbit until he's ready to throw you over his shoulder and take you to bed. Then he'll profess his undying love and whisk you into the sunset."

"That sounds horrible."

She giggles. "Does it really, though? Last I checked, he's your type. I'm pretty sure he wrote the book on your type. In fact, he might be the only page in the book."

My brain smugly supplies me with an image of my decimated sketchbook to validate her words, but like the stubborn fool I am, I double down. "My life rules aren't going to magically change in six months, Kel. You know I don't do relationships. I'm perfectly happy alone."

"I know, Soph. Just like I know you have good reasons for being a terminal skeptic." She squeezes my hands. "Maybe after hanging out with him a few more times, you'll realize he's a giant douche and never want to talk to him again."

"Doubtful," I mutter. "He's surprisingly hard not to like."

She laughs. "I don't doubt it. Remember that day, when I was all ready to bash him over the head? Then, when you tried to blame yourself for what happened, he wouldn't let you. He took accountability, apologized, then offered to let you kick him in the balls. He's like a unicorn. Golden retriever energy with a ginormous di—"

"I remember! Don't remind me. *Ugh*."

She laughs as she leans back. "You're really not going to tell him you've met before?"

"What would be the point? There's no way he remembers."

"I bet he does."

I knuckle my forehead. Kelly polishes off her danish in silence, letting me stew. Eventually, I drop my head onto my arms. The bell on the door rings. Kelly nudges my foot with hers. I nudge her back.

"I should have just slept with him after bowling," I whine. "Before he made that stupid bet with Rose."

Kelly gasps and kicks me at the same time. I whip my head up to see her staring over my head.

Molten horror climbs up my spine and gives me a head rush. "Tell me it's not him," I beg. She makes a garbled noise in her throat.

"Dollface!" comes a low, teasing voice right behind me. "I'm appalled. You would've taken advantage of me and ruined our blossoming friendship?"

A second later, Matt makes himself comfortable in a chair at our table. He smiles at Kelly. "Hi, I'm Matt." Then he frowns a little. "You look familiar, have we met?"

I spear Kelly with a death glare until she says, "Kelly, nice to meet you. Nope, don't think we've met." Her smile while they shake hands is too big and false, but Matt doesn't seem to notice.

His eyes veer to me, sparkling with mischief. "I was in the neighborhood and thought I'd visit my bestie at work. How's your day going?"

"Fine," I say, my voice strangled. "How's yours?"

He grins at my obvious discomfort. "Just peachy." He turns to Kelly. "Are you her other best friend? Do we need to agree on a custody arrangement?"

Kelly laughs, utterly charmed. I can't even blame her. "I don't think that will be necessary. Although, I should probably tell you that you're not invited to our bi-weekly movie night. It's girls only."

Matt chuckles. "Fair enough." He turns that penetrating blue gaze back on me. I can't help noticing his hair is messier than usual, like he just rolled out of bed. "What are you doing Friday night?"

"I work. Why?"

"What time do you get off?"

"Usually nine-thirty, sometimes later. Depends on the mess made at open mic night. Why?"

"Are you super tired after work, or do you feel up for doing something late?"

"Depends. *Why*, Matt?"

Kelly's eyes tick from side to side like she's viewing a tennis match, a little smile on her face.

Matt drags a hand over his jaw. "Shit, this is harder than I thought it would be."

I frown. "What is?" To my astonishment, his cheekbones tint a few shakes darker. My jaw drops. "Are you... are you blushing?" I look at Kelly. "Are you seeing this?"

She cackles. "Totally seeing this."

He groans. "Give me a break, ladies. This feels a bit like asking Jenna Callahan to the eighth grade dance again."

"But you're not dating Sophie," chirps Kelly. Her grin has a maniacal tilt to it. "You're *friends*."

Matt gets ahold of himself with a little laugh. "Let me try this again." He clears his throat and pins me with his gaze. "Nick is having a get-together at his house Friday night. I thought maybe you'd want to come? Nothing crazy, maybe twenty or thirty people. It will be our first official friend date. Non-date. Rendezvous? Whatever."

It sounds like a nightmare.

Kelly kicks my shin so hard I wince.

"Sure," I hear my voice say. "Sounds like fun."

WHEN I GET HOME that evening, I putter around my apartment, filling minutes with mindless tasks. I throw in a load of laundry. Pop the top on one of Matt's beers and drink it too fast. Do the dishes, wipe the kitchen counters. Organize the chaos on my kitchen table. Turn on some music—which I turn back off when the first track on the playlist is a Breaking Giants's song.

By midnight, the urge to grab my sketchbook and recreate the look on Matt's face when he blushed is nigh overpowering.

Refusing to give in to the temptation, I wander into my bathroom. Before I'm fully conscious of what I'm doing, I've plugged the bathtub and cranked on the water.

I haven't taken a bath in almost eight years, despite my apartment boasting a prized, full-sized tub. I take my clothes off anyway, then spool my hair into a bun and secure it with a clip. I even unearth a candle and lighter from beneath the sink.

Pickle meows his way into the bathroom as I'm lighting the candle. He curls up on the bathmat and watches me drop lavender-scented bath oil in the water, a gift from my mom a few Christmases ago, unopened until tonight.

"Don't give me that look," I tell him as I turn off the water. He squints at me, then licks his paw and swipes it over an ear.

I turn off the overhead light and stare at the bath. Steam rises. The water ripples under candlelight. Minutes pass. My legs tremble beneath me.

"Pull it together, Soph," I tell myself. "Get in the fucking bathtub."

It takes me another few minutes to put one foot in. Another minute passes before the other joins it. Breathing shallowly through my nose, I slowly lower into the water. It's barely hot anymore, but I don't notice, sitting rigidly with half of me submerged.

I should have left the light on. The water is too dark under a single candle flame. Panic tingles along the edges of me, gaining density and purpose. Memory surges, rising over my head, poised to drown me.

I yelp as Pickle's face pops over the rim of the tub. He whacks the water. A smile pulls at my mouth as he stares at his paw like he's never seen it before, then shakes it like a maraca.

"Water," I inform him. He chirrups and whacks the surface again. Panic recedes, and my breathing evens out.

Pickle wasn't the one who saved my life eight years ago—that was Josh—but he's saved me a thousand times in other ways. Like he's saving me right now. From memory, from the darkest parts of myself.

Stretching out my legs under the water, I lean back, finally relaxing. Lavender-scented air wraps around me. Pickle continues battling the forces of evil in the water. Smiling, I rub the soft fur between his pointed ears. He leans into my touch and purrs, which reminds me of the lie I told Matt last night.

My cat is picky as fuck about who touches him, and until yesterday, he only purred for me.

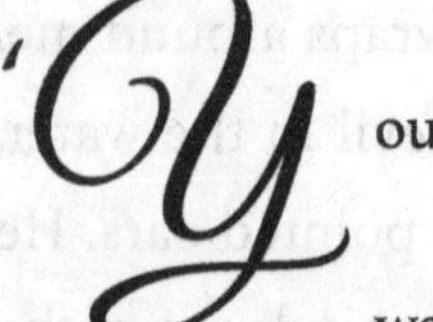 ou can't wear that."

I gape at the man crowding my doorway. "You did *not* just say that."

Matt's expression is pained. "That came out wrong. What I meant to say is you'll feel overdressed. I'm just looking out for you. As a friend."

I look down at my black dress. It's not fancy or anything, just a basic long-sleeved, body-hugging style that hits me below my knees. No cleavage on display. I'm wearing sneakers and a puffy jacket with it, for fuck's sake.

On the other hand, Matt is in tattered jeans and hooded sweatshirt. And he does look sincere.

"Fine," I say, waving him into my apartment. "Give me a minute."

Five minutes later, I return to the living room to find Matt sprawled on the couch. Pickle sits on his chest, head butting his chin and purring.

"That's a good little beastie," Matt murmurs as he scratches behind Pickle's ears. "Yes, you are. You love me, don't you?"

I clear my throat, and both cat and man look at me like I caught them doing something they shouldn't. "Better?" I ask, waving to my ensemble of jeans, T-shirt, chunky cardigan, and combat boots.

Matt grins, nodding, and sets Pickle aside. "You look great. Cozy and cute. And that sweater matches your eyes. I want to wrap you in a blanket and make you hot cocoa."

I grimace. "Bleh."

He laughs as he rounds the couch. Eyes sparkling down at me, he tugs a strand of my loose hair. "You hate compliments so much. It's funny. You're... funny." The word trips a little in his mouth, making it sound like he was going to say something else. He clears his throat. "All set? How are you feeling? Do you need food, or do you want to stop and grab a coffee somewhere?"

I sigh in mingled humor and exasperation. "I work in a coffee shop, remember? I had a double espresso before leaving tonight. And I ate. Stop babying me. It's annoying."

He grins and gestures toward the front door. "After you."

I give Pickle a treat, make sure he has water, then lock up behind us. Matt leads me to a surprisingly normal-looking SUV parked in my building's guest parking. I stare at it in confusion.

"Why the weird face?" he asks, chuckling as he unlocks the car and opens the passenger door for me. "Let me guess, you thought I'd be driving some obnoxious sports car."

"Pretty much."

I climb inside and buckle up. Matt slides into the driver's seat and throws me a bland look. "Did it occur to you that money doesn't necessarily change who a person is?"

I smile. "Nope."

He snorts, navigating out of the parking lot and toward the main road. "Well, consider this your first lesson. I cook for myself, my clothes are off the rack, and I've had this car for over six years. I even do my own laundry and clean my own house."

I stop myself before saying, *No, you don't,* but can't help throwing out, "You seriously clean? I don't believe it."

"Believe whatever you want, Dollface." He hesitates. "I'm not saying my house is pristine or anything.

Or that I enjoy mopping and vacuuming. But who does?"

"Why, though?" I press. "I say if you have the money, get a cleaning service. Shit, I would if I could afford it. Not having to scrub a toilet ever again? Sign me up."

He's silent for a few seconds, concentrating on the road. "I did actually use a service. Exactly once. Back in those young and dumb days. I'll never do it again."

I freeze in my seat.

Oh my God, he does remember.

"That sounds ominous. What, uh, happened?"

He glances at me, then laughs a little. "It's super embarrassing, actually. I'm not sure I want to tell you."

"Now I have to know."

I'm dying to know, actually.

Matt sighs in surrender. "Some friends of mine back then decided to bring a party to the house I was renting. I shouldn't even say friends, actually. Just some people who hung around the band. I didn't even like them that much.

"When I finally kicked them out, the place was trashed. There was freaking puke everywhere. On the floors, in the plants. So much garbage. Mounds of cigarette butts." He shudders. "I freaked out and called our manager, who chewed me out for waking him up, then chewed me out for being an idiot. He said he'd bail me out one time and one time only, called me a bunch more names, then told me to go to sleep."

"I think I like him."

Matt laughs. "Yeah, Phil's awesome. He basically raised four wild, punk-ass kids. I think we're the reason he has gray hair nowadays. Anyway, I didn't hear anything back, so I went to bed."

My heart starts racing. "And?"

"And sometime the next morning, two ladies showed up and started cleaning. One of them came in the bedroom while I was still asleep..." He trails off, fingers tightening on the steering wheel, his jaw clenching.

"It can't be that bad," I say, my voice thready. "What happened?"

"I take it back—it's not embarrassing, it's fucking shameful. I don't want you to think I'm okay with what happened. I'm really, really not." He glances at me quickly; I see his throat move as he swallows. "It was dark and she came near the bed. I woke up and heard her, and I thought it was my girlfriend at the time. I... I grabbed this poor girl and pulled her onto the bed."

We're at a stop light, and I watch him close his eyes for long seconds, expression twisted in conflict.

"I didn't take off her clothes or anything, but I basi-cally assaulted her," he continues in a low voice. "She was frozen. Trembling. When I realized what was happening, I apologized profusely, but shit... it still haunts me. I ended up telling my manager, who told our publicist, who called our lawyer. Long story short, they made her sign an NDA."

I can't take it anymore.

"Matt, you didn't assault her."

The light turns green and he accelerates onto the freeway. "I appreciate that, but you're just trying to make me feel better. You weren't there."

I suck in a lungful of air and let it out in a rush. "Yes, I was. I was the girl you grabbed. You recognized Kelly on Monday because it was her cleaning service. I was helping her out that day. You didn't assault me."

Maybe dropping the bomb while surrounded by cars going sixty miles an hour isn't the smartest move of my life, but it works in my favor. Matt stays hyper focused on the road, his expression blank.

"Matt?"

"Give me a minute," he says hoarsely.

I stay tense and quiet, and when five minutes pass without him speaking, I eventually turn to stare out the window.

When he takes an exit, I half expect him to circle back to the freeway and take me home, but he keeps driving. He doesn't seem mad, exactly, just very contained. I wish I knew what he was thinking, but I keep my mouth shut. I know what it's like to need time to process.

Eventually, the houses start getting bigger, the trees older and taller. Nick's house is easy to spot: there are cars spilling out of the driveway and parked at the curbs to either side.

Matt pulls against an empty stretch of curb and parks, though he doesn't turn off the engine.

"You look completely different," he says finally. "Like... *completely* different."

"Yeah, I do. No more glasses, no more dyed hair, a lot more tattoos." I was also too thin, had bad skin, and carried dark circles under my eyes like it was my job.

I feel his stare and make myself turn toward him. He watches me with an expression I still can't read, but it's closer to confusion than anger.

"Is that why you avoided me like the plague when I saw you at Josh's studio? Why you'd barely look at me at Tullamore that night?"

The car suddenly feels too small, the space between us not nearly wide enough. "Possibly. You're also Matt Sullivan from Breaking Giants, in case you forgot."

He rolls his eyes. "Like you give a shit about that."

It makes my lips twitch. "You're not mad I didn't tell you?"

He shakes his head. "Why would I be mad? Besides,

I've been carrying around guilt for six years, and you're the angel who just took it off my shoulders." He pauses. "You swear you're telling me the truth? I didn't scar you for life that day?"

I huff out a laugh. "No, Matt. It was definitely jarring in the moment, but when you realized I wasn't your girlfriend, you literally catapulted off the bed in the opposite direction. You were just as horrified as I was."

"But..." He sighs and shakes his head, like he still doesn't believe me. "You were so scared. White as a sheet. I remember that clearly."

Following impulse, I grab his nearest hand. He jerks in surprise, then returns my squeeze. "Listen to me very carefully, Matthew. Wait—your name is actually Matthew, right?"

His lips quirk, eyes flaring with humor. "Yes, Sophie. But only my mom and my best friend are allowed to call me that."

I bite my cheek against the urge to laugh. "Okay, then. Listen, Matthew. You didn't hurt me. It wasn't violent. You basically cuddled me." *And humped my ass with your giant erection,* but I decide to leave that part out. "You realized your mistake, immediately let me go, and apologized. No one made me sign the NDA—I did it willingly."

"Promise?" he whispers.

My heart thumps hard. I release his hand, the contact abruptly too much. His question, his reaction—then and now—serve as stark reminders of *why* I know he doesn't deserve to carry any guilt. And why others should, but don't.

"Yes. I promise."

He releases a heavy sigh and scrapes his hands through his hair. "Shit. This is intense. I feel like we stepped to the next level in the Best Friend Game."

Light pierces the darkness of my mind, clearing away the shadows as a laugh floats past my lips.

"For the record," he says cheekily, "for those five seconds six years ago, you were pretty awesome to cuddle."

I punch his arm. "Dumbass."

Laughing, we get out of the car.

12

The first thing I see when we walk into Nick's house is a group of three women in revealing dresses lounging on a couch. My black dress covered twice as much skin. In fact, as my gaze scans the open-concept main floor and the clusters of people, I realize Matt and I are underdressed in comparison to everyone else.

I launch my elbow into his stomach, barely denting hard muscle. He grunts and rubs the area. "Dang, Doll-face. What was that for?"

I jerk my head toward the women. "What the hell, dude?" I hiss.

He looks at them in confusion. Then understanding dawns, along with a grimace. "Sorry?" He doesn't actually sound sorry; he sounds amused.

Before I can say anything else, Rose appears in the hallway. She grins when she sees us and hurries our way. Her maxi dress is loose around the waist, but as she moves, I catch the small but distinct bulge of her abdomen. Her fingers unconsciously skate over the area.

Guess she finally took a test.

"Hey, Matty!" She launches into his arms, squeezing him around the middle.

"Hey, Rosie Posie," he replies, patting the springy curls on her head. "How's it going?"

"Super good."

Rose releases him and turns her vibrating energy toward me. There's a second when she starts to lean toward me, as if to give me a hug, but Matt shifts his body slightly between us.

"How's the tadpole?" he asks, diverting her attention.

Happiness radiates from Rose as she rubs a hand over her tummy. "The little bugger is taking it easy on me today." She looks at me and winces. "Sorry again about—"

"No worries at all," I interject quickly. "I still remember what my mom was like when she was pregnant with my sister. It was a rollercoaster."

Rose laughs. "You're too nice. Well, everyone is out back at the moment. I'm headed to the bathroom for the tenth time this hour."

"TMI, Rose," Matt mutters.

She just grins and with a little wave, disappears down the hallway.

"Thanks," I murmur. "For the interference."

He smiles softly. "I've got your back. Come on, let's go see what's going on outside. It's too stuffy in here, anyway."

His words make no sense. The house is spacious. It's not terribly crowded either, maybe fifteen people spread across the open-concept living area. Then I realize the roughly half that are women are surreptitiously—or in a few cases, boldly—eyeing us. More accurately, they're eyeballing *him*, with only small, scathing glances being periodically sent my way.

My skin crawls lightly, but I purposely latch onto the hilarity of the circumstance. "This is why you wanted me to come, isn't it? To be your bodyguard and keep all the rabid women at bay so you're not tempted to lose your precious bet? Low, Matthew. So low."

He laughs. "Of course not. Don't be ridiculous." He walks down the hallway and I follow. As he pushes through the back door, he winks over his shoulder. "It's just a perk."

There's about the same number of people spread outside, but it seems more crowded, most of them clus-tered under an overhang on outdoor furniture. Two space heaters provide a toasty counterpoint to the cool night air. Everyone is talking, laughing, seemingly friends or at least, friendly.

I feel my body responding to the unfamiliar environment, unfamiliar faces. Tension ripples down my legs. I want badly to grab Matt's hand and get the fuck out of here, but before I can, his gaze lands on my face. Heavy, searching.

"I won't leave you," he says softly. "Here, come on."

He guides me to an outdoor fridge, snags two beers, and pops their tops, then hands one to me. I take it gratefully and manage a small sip.

"There he is!" yells Nick, and suddenly, a dozen sets of eyes are staring our way. A myriad of voices call out greetings. I shrink behind Matt, close enough that his scent wraps around me, inexplicably calming.

"Get your ass over here, poster-boy!" someone says loudly. "Julian won't play for us and we demand entertainment!"

Matt laughs. "Quit whining, Troy."

"I'm not a dancing monkey," adds Julian. The words are without rancor, and a handful of people start making monkey sounds, which makes everyone else laugh, including Julian.

I peer around Matt to see Breaking Giants's frontman sitting on a couch beside Nick and his wife,

Kat. Julian's eyes dart to the back door, and a huge smile overtakes his face. Glancing back, I see Rose coming outside. Feeling like a voyeur, I look away, but my chest warms. I don't know Julian, but his reaction to his pregnant wife just earned a million brownie points from me.

Rose weaves through people and settles on the couch beside him. He wraps an arm around her shoulders and murmurs something in her ear. She smiles, small and private, then her eyes find Matt in the crowd.

"I'll sing if you play, Matty. Only one song, though, because Julian and I are heading home in a few."

There's a chorus of whistles and a few laughs. Rose rolls her eyes, but Julian whispers something to her again and her cheeks flush.

Matt looks at me before answering. Feeling the press of inquisitive gazes, I say quickly, "Go."

A line appears between his brows. "Are you sure?"

"Matthew Sullivan," I hiss, "if you don't stop babying me, I'm going to call in that promise you made me six years ago."

Blue eyes cloud with confusion, which clears after a moment and shifts to amusement. His lips tilt in a crooked grin. "I said you could kick me in the balls, didn't I?"

I nod and give him a light shove. Thankfully, he doesn't resist, and a minute later, he's settling on the couch beside Rose. Someone hands him a guitar, taking his beer in exchange. He and Rose trade soft words.

"So, are you Matt's new girl?" asks a voice to my left.

"Nope, just a friend." I take a sip of beer and glance quickly at the speaker: male, average height, dark-haired, good-looking. From my brief assessment of his expression, though, I kind of wish I'd said yes.

"Nice. I'm Sam."

I nod, a short jerk. "Sophie. Nice to meet you."

Sam opens his mouth, but thankfully closes it again as the first chords from Matt's guitar ripple in the air. The whole patio goes quiet. Rose sits forward beside him, a half-smile on her lips.

After a few more testing chords and a tweak of tuning, Matt's whole body *changes*. I watch, rapt, as the air around him seems to charge. His features tighten, then relax. His eyes drift half-closed.

And then he plays.

We all recognize the intro to the song "Over The Hills And Far Away" by Led Zeppelin. A few low whistles sound, because this isn't a random person with a hobby playing guitar, and Breaking Giants isn't just famous for their pretty faces. Matt is a true talent.

He adds flares that make the familiar tune somehow *more*. There's emotion in every note, his long fingers moving swiftly over the chords and neck, too fast and skilled for my non-musical brain to comprehend.

I'm not the only one whose mouth is open in dazed awe.

Right on cue, Rose starts singing. Her voice is liquid. Perfect. Her range is stunning. But I can't stop staring at Matt, the way his shoulders move, the way his thigh flexes as he taps out a rhythm.

At some point, I realize he's been watching me watch him. Aware that I probably look starstruck, I don't even attempt to hide the blush that heats my face. Though I do roll my eyes. His lips curve slightly, his gaze darkening in a way that sends delayed, heated pulses down my body.

Finally, his stare drops as his concentration returns to the song's culmination.

Beside me, Sam murmurs, "See you around, Sophie," and disappears.

I try not to read into the knowing tone in his voice.

But my heart pounds, anyway.

Matt doesn't ghost me again; nor do we talk every day. Nevertheless, by the end of our first month of friendship, he's a consistent presence in my life.

So far, we've gone to another show at a local venue, watched a movie at my apartment, and last week, we went to an after-hours roller rink. It was a group outing: Nick, Kat, Jackson, and Christina came, and I invited Kelly and a few of our other friends—who thankfully managed to keep their cool around the rock stars.

It was the most fun I've had in ages, despite the bruises lingering on my ass.

The pockets of time wherein Matt and I don't text or call—a day here, two days there—keep my head level. We don't hug, we fist bump. We don't flirt, and except for his one-off, occasionally salacious compliments that I've learned to laugh off, we don't acknowledge the heat that charges the air when we get too close.

Denial has become my middle name.

Only in bed at night do I allow myself to feel the increasing demand in my body. The craving for his hands and mouth. Sometimes I give in, using my trusty vibrator to take the edge off. Sometimes, too, when I'm so frustrated I could scream, I pull up dating apps and browse for a hookup.

I never swipe right, though.

And I refuse to admit why.

"GET OFF YOUR ASS AND HELP," growls Josh as we pass the couch, our arms laden with totes full of groceries.

Patrick doesn't look up from his phone. "You guys can handle it. I believe in you."

I shoulder open the door to the kitchen and dump my bags on the island. "Give him a break, Josh. He took out the trash when we asked him, too, didn't he?"

Josh's scowl stays fixed as he drops his burden in front of the fridge. "We were basically adults at nineteen. He's a giant waste of space."

I start unpacking the closest totes. "But wouldn't it

have been nice to *not* be adults at that age? We can't resent Patrick for not having our burdens. Especially since we're the reason he didn't have to grow up as fast as us."

He sighs and pulls open the fridge. "You're right. As usual. It just rubs me wrong sometimes."

I don't say anything. We've had this conversation and others like it enough times over the years for me to know the issue can't be solved with words. Josh's baggage is different from mine—even if I can name it, I can't carry it for him.

When our stepdad split, I was thirteen and Josh was fifteen. Our mom was grieving the jackass's abandonment while dealing with a newborn Beka and her health issues. Patrick was only three, and Josh and I immediately picked up the slack, becoming his surrogate parents. Feeding him, bathing him, putting him to bed. Taking him to our neighbor Claudia to watch while we were at school. Picking him up when the bus brought us home.

As Beka's health—and our mom's sanity—stabilized, things eventually slid back into the realm of "normal." I didn't have a problem transitioning back into a big sister role with Patrick. Josh, on the other hand, continued to straddle the line between brother and parental figure as the years went on. Despite the Herculean efforts of our mom to lighten his emotional load, Josh held firmly to his role as Man of the House.

Patrick loves Josh, potentially more than he does any of us, but he's old enough now to buck against his brother's self-prescribed role as a father figure. Josh, on the other hand, sees Patrick's general laziness and lack of focus in life as his fault.

As I finish unbagging and start putting away the groceries, my phone vibrates in my back pocket with an incoming call. My stupid stomach flutters. I haven't spoken to Matt in a day. *Calm down. It might not be him.*

I pull it out and see his face on the screen—a selfie he took on my phone and attached to his contact info. He's holding Pickle next to his face and grinning like a kid with a cookie. My cat looks annoyed as fuck. It makes me laugh every time I see it.

"Hi, Matthew."

"Hi back, Dollface. What are you wearing?"

I smirk. "A garbage bag."

"Ohh, sexy." I can hear the smile in his voice. "And how are you this fine Thursday afternoon?"

"Good. I'm at my mom's. Josh and I just did a Costco and grocery store run. We're unloading now." I pause. "If you're calling because you want to hang out today, I'm going to be here for a while. Until after dinner, at least."

"Maybe I just wanted to hear your voice."

I open my mouth, but no words come out.

Thankfully he continues lightly, "Nah, you're right. I wanted to see my bestie. Give me a call when you're headed home?"

"Sure," I choke out.

"Okay, then. Say hi to Josh for me. Talk to you later."

"Bye."

The call ends and I tuck my phone back in my pocket.

"*Matthew*?" asks Josh, staring at me over the fridge door with a glint in his eye. "Was that who I think it was?"

"Uhh, yeah. Matt." I clear my throat and busy myself with separating dry goods and produce. "I told you we've become friends. We hang out sometimes. It's no big deal."

"Uh-huh. Then explain why your face is bright red."

"It's hot as hell in here. You know Mom overdoes it on the heat."

Josh bites his lips and shakes his head slowly. "Shit, sis. This is not good."

"What? What's not good?" I fill my arms with various boxes and head for the pantry. "What are you even talking about?"

Josh follows me, his voice lowering with urgency. "Sophie, listen to me. Whatever is happening between you and Matt, it needs to stop. I've known Matt for a long time. He's a good dude, but he's not boyfriend material."

I jerk around to face him. "Who said anything about boyfriends? Do you even know me? We're *friends*, Josh. Am I not allowed to have them?"

He grimaces. "You're deluding yourself. There's no way Matt just wants to be your friend." His jaw hardens. "This is fucked up, actually. I told him you were off-limits."

Anger sparks in my bloodstream. "Excuse me? You *what*? Since when is it any of your business who I spend my time with?"

He throws both hands up. "Hey, don't get mad at me. I'm just trying to protect you."

The volcano inside me explodes.

"Well, stop! I'm not Patrick, so don't talk to me like you're my fucking dad!" I regret the words instantly, sickness flashing in my gut. His face whitens. "Josh—"

"Forget it," he snaps, turning away. "Get your heart trampled by Matt. I don't care. Live your life, learn your lessons. But I won't be there to pull your ass from the fire this time."

"Josh, wait. Please!"

The kitchen door slams behind him, then the front door. His car starts with a muted growl, which fades as he drives away. I press a hand to my churning stomach, fighting tears.

Goddammit.

Patrick stands on the other side of the island, his hand inside a bag of chips. "That was intense. Family, huh?"

"Grow up, Patrick," I snap, then sigh and rub my forehead. "Sorry."

"All good." He glances around at the groceries half put away. "Want me to take care of this?"

The burn at the back of my eyes intensifies. I muster a smile. "Yeah, thanks. I'm gonna head home, okay? Tell Mom we'll raincheck dinner. Don't tell her about the fight, though. She'll just worry."

He nods, gaze roaming the island and snagging on a box of pasta and cans of tomato sauce. "Were you gonna do lasagna?"

"Yeah," I say weakly.

He rolls up the bag of chips. "I can handle it. I've watched you guys make it a thousand times. Beka knows how, too, and she'll be home from school soon. We've got this, Soph."

A tear leaks from my eye. Taking three steps to his side, I wrap my arms around his slender middle.

"Whoa, there," he says with a laugh. "Now you're freaking me out."

I squeeze him tighter. "I love you, Patrick. Even when you're being a little shit to Josh."

Huffing a short laugh, he finally hugs me back. "I swear it's not on purpose. Most of the time, at least." He sighs into my hair. "I know how much you guys do for us. And I love you, too."

I squeeze him tighter. "I love you, Barrie. I love when you're being a little shit to Josh."

Hiding a short laugh, he finally hugs me back. "I swear it's not on purpose. Most of the time, at least. He gets into my head. Know how much you guys do for us. And I love you, too."

14

───────

In addition to adding a photo to his contact info on my phone, Matt inputted his address. I drive there in a fog, following directions on autopilot. I don't even know if he's home right now.

Every so often, lightning-bright thoughts flash through the gloom in my head, zapping me with Josh's words, his concern, and the horrible thing I said to him. He didn't deserve that.

Because he's right.

I have to stop this.

Matt lives less than five miles from Nick. I pull into the driveway and park behind his SUV, then lean forward to gape at the house.

Two stories, rich navy with white trim, it has a garden and small yard in front, a wide porch, and a second-level balcony with two chairs and a little table. Given the size of the lots on either side and the glimpse of giant trees over the roof, it has a decent swath of land in the back. The location alone—within four blocks of Lake Washington—tells me the price tag is in the millions.

I drop my head to the steering wheel. I don't belong here, in this world of mansions, charming brick pathways, and teak patio furniture.

Movement in my peripheral brings my head up. Matt stands beside my car, wearing sweatpants and a thin T-shirt. No shoes. Goose bumps ripple down his arms. His phone is in one hand. He doesn't look the least bit surprised to see me.

I roll down my window. "Josh called you?" I guess.

He nods, then glances up at the gray sky, darker than it should be at 3:00 p.m. "It's about to dump. Come on. I just made some coffee."

Sighing, I turn off the car and follow him inside. The heavy front door closes with a thump that seals the fact I'm out of my element. Everything around me screams quality, from the hardwood floors to the paint colors and light fixtures. To my left is a room with an entire wall of built-in bookshelves, every row filled with colorful spines. The rest of the space is taken up by a giant grand piano, glistening and dust-free.

On my right is a sitting room. Beautiful brick fireplace, two leather couches facing each other over a coffee table with a cluster of unlit candles on it. Muted pillows, a cashmere throw blanket, a giant cream area rug. Well-tended plants frame the picture window. Actual art—not prints—hangs from the walls. Everything is clean. Visually perfect.

"Take a breath, Dollface. The furniture won't kill you."

I want to explain. To tell him why. *Why* it's so hard for me. *Why* what didn't bother me when we were at Nick's house is bothering me now.

Maybe I will today. The truth will send him running.

"It's so clean in there because I never use that room," he says like he can read my mind. "Come to the kitchen."

Numb, I follow his broad back down a hallway, the rich wood creaking under our steps. Vents funnel heat onto our legs. We turn through a wide archway and Matt gestures me to a butcher-block kitchen table. I sit, barely feeling the surface of the bench beneath me. He veers around a beautiful marble island to pull mugs from a cabinet. At least there are signs of clutter around me: reusable tote bags on a peg, papers on the island under his wallet and keys, a water glass near the sink.

Another large archway leads to a living room with a

giant, wall-mounted flat-screen. More couches, cozy chairs, and floating shelves with leaning art and knick-knacks. Though the aesthetic is cohesive—earthy warmth and soothing neutrals—it doesn't have the sterile vibe of the sitting room. There are shoes on the floor and a sweatshirt thrown over the arm of a couch. An empty beer bottle on the coffee table. Two guitars sit on stands against one wall. One of the stands is crooked.

"Here."

An un-chipped mug is set before me; by the color of the coffee, I know he added just the right amount of cream for me. I take a sip, hoping the warmth will unthaw my voice, which is frozen somewhere in my chest.

Matt sits down across from me. "Josh isn't wrong, you know," he murmurs. "If you were my sister, I'd warn you away from me, too."

My eyes flash up to his, then quickly away. They're too blue right now; they see too much.

He laughs softly, without a trace of humor. "Why does it feel like you're about to friend-dump me?"

My voice finally thaws. "I'm considering it."

"Why?" he asks flatly.

I think about what Rose said weeks ago, and about the way I catch him looking at me sometimes—like I'm the answer to some unfathomable question in his life. I think about Kelly's prediction for how our stupid friend experiment will end.

"Maybe I don't want to hurt you," I whisper.

The silence is weighted, both of us unmoving. At length, Matt says, "I don't think this is about me. I think it's about you and what you're afraid of."

I'm no longer frozen; his words stoke the same fire Josh stuck his hand in earlier. "Oh, really? Tell me, then. What am I afraid of?"

Expression guarded, he shrugs. "Give me a little credit. I'm not stupid. Someone hurt you badly. A boyfriend, I'm guessing. You don't trust men, and you definitely don't trust whatever this is between you and me."

"And what exactly *is* this?" I demand.

"Why do we have to put it in a box? We're friends." His eyes narrow, glittering darkly, and his voice drops to a tense growl. "I think what you really want to ask me is if I jack off thinking about you on my cock. You already know the answer to that question, Sophie. Every fucking day."

A different type of heat explodes inside me. I drop my head into my hands. A hysterical laugh clogs my throat. I want to launch over the table at him, but I don't know if it's to slap his face or tear off his clothes.

"As for hurting me," he continues in the same dark

tone, "I'm a big boy and can take care of myself. As of right now, I want you as my friend more than I want you in my bed. Friendship, like all relationships, is about communication and trust. Have I done anything to make you feel unsafe with me? To make you think you can't trust me?"

"No," I whisper.

"So here's a question for you: do you like hanging out with me? Do we get along?"

"Yes."

"Can you deal with me being attracted to you? Which, I'll remind you, shouldn't be the least bit shocking."

"I don't know, Matt. It's... confusing."

"Why?" he demands.

I throw my hands up. "Does there have to be a why?"

His jaw clenches, and it occurs to me I've never seen him mad before. And definitely not at me. It makes his eyes darker, more stormy sea than sky.

I blurt, "Are we having our first fight?"

His lips twitch, then harden again. Leaning forward, he traps me in his gaze. "We're not fighting. We're having an impassioned discussion about honesty in our friendship. And you're purposely redirecting. Tell me the truth, Sophie. Just say it."

"Fine!" I choke out. "I'm attracted to you, too, okay? I

want you. *Badly*. But I also haven't had sex in over six months, so it doesn't mean—"

"Stop," he snaps, then deflates, dragging a hand through his hair. He stares at his cooling coffee, his gaze blank, mind a thousand miles away. "It's not your fault."

Cold suddenly, I wrap my arms around myself. "What are you talking about?"

When he looks up, I flinch at the pain in his eyes. "Do you know why I came up with that stupid experiment?"

"The bet with Rose."

He laughs, low and bitter. "No. Because my ex told me she wasn't enough for me, and that I'd prove her right when I fucked the first pretty woman to give me the time of day."

I suck in a breath. "That's harsh."

He snorts. "She could be the queen of harsh, that one. She was fond of reminding me that my need for physical affirmations from women—AKA sex—stems from the fact my father walked out on my mom. It's me being like him: constantly seeking what makes me feel like a bigger man."

"Holy shit," I whisper.

"I never cheated on her," he says, a muscle in his jaw jumping. "I never wanted to. Not once. I *loved* her. She also told me I wasn't enough for her, either, so there's that. Two sides to every story, you know? She's not the villain like Rose and Julian think. We shared the role. And I think... maybe the truth hurts sometimes. And she was always brutally honest."

"There's a difference between honesty and cruelty. What she said about you, about your dad—that was cruel, Matt."

"Maybe. Maybe not. It doesn't matter." His eyes flash to mine. "I didn't tell you that so you'd feel sorry for me."

I know why he told me. He wants me to open up to him, too. Offer my pain like he offered his.

"Matt..." My eyes burn again. *Don't cry, don't fucking cry.* "I do trust you. In the last month, you've become one of my closest friends. But not even all my friends know what happened. Why I'm so fucked up. Has it occurred to you that maybe I don't want to tell you because it will change the way you look at me? You might not even want to be friends anymore."

"Not gonna happen," he says, then sighs. "But I hear you. It's not fair of me to ask you to show me your scars." I flinch, but thankfully he's staring at the table again. "I don't... I don't know why I feel this insane need to know your secrets. I'm sorry." Self-deprecating laugh. "My ex would probably say I'm seeking a substitute for the sex I've sworn off. Something to give me the illusion of power or control."

His apology and the fucked-up explanation slice right through my emotional scar tissue. Darkness leaks like ink inside me.

I shove up the sleeves of my sweater and stretch my arms over the table, palms up. "Look, Matt."

He gives me a questioning glance. I shake my fists on the table, drawing his gaze down.

The tattoos Josh placed over the scars make them almost invisible. It takes Matt a solid seven seconds—I count them—before the blood drains from his face.

"Sophie," he whispers brokenly. His hands instinctively reach for me. I yank my arms back to my sides, pulling down my sleeves.

"Still want to be my friend?"

His eyes widen, then narrow. "Why the fuck would you say that?"

I blow out a breath. "Sorry."

Matt stands up. "You're shaking. Will you come with me, please? Let's at least sit somewhere more comfortable."

He hovers as I stand up, eyeing me like I'm fragile and might fall and break. *Exactly why I don't tell people.* Annoyed, I brush past him and walk into the living room, dropping into the corner of the couch.

A second later, a blanket smacks me in the face. I pull it down and glare. "What the hell?"

He smiles slightly. "Just matching your energy."

My irritation melts away. Rolling my eyes, I cuddle under the blanket, fighting the desire to smell it the way he smelled mine.

Matt plops onto the other side of the couch. "Okay. So you had an accident with a sharp knife. Failed out of culinary school?"

Against my will, I laugh, which makes him grin, albeit softly. "Bad joke, man. Really bad."

"I know," he murmurs. "It was either that or try to hug you, and I like my balls where they are."

I bite my lip. "I guess you want to know all the dirty details, huh?"

He shakes his head, eyes screwing closed. "You only showed me because I was pushing you so hard." A hand rubs over his chest like the area hurts. "Jesus, maybe you *should* kick me in the balls."

I sigh in mingled affection and sadness. *This freaking man.* Before I can talk myself out of it, I slide across the couch and lift his arm. His eyes pop open, wide with shock, as I settle against his side and let his arm drop over my shoulder.

God, it feels good being this close to him. Warm. Safe. I rest my head on his chest and smile at the sound of his stampeding heart.

"Relax, Matthew. I don't bite."

His muscles unclench in increments. Legs, then stomach. Chest, and finally shoulders. His heartbeat slows. His arm tightens marginally around me. There's a light pressure on my head, his nose or maybe lips, there and gone.

A sense of peace filters through me.

I take a deep breath, and then I tell him the truth.

15

"**W**hat's wrong with you, man? You've been missing cues all day."

I blink at Jackson. He, Nick, and Julian are watching me with varying levels of irritation and concern.

"Sorry," I mumble. "Haven't been sleeping well."

"Let's take a break," Julian offers. When the door of his home studio closes behind Jackson and Nick, he pushes aside his mic. "Talk to me."

I shake my head and set my guitar on its stand. "I'm fine, really. Just not sleeping. I'll go get some coffee and we can try again."

"*Matt.*"

I wince at his tone, which carries the weight of our decade-plus of friendship. There's no one who knows me as well as he does. He's closer than a brother to me.

I'd bury any body Jackson or Nick needed me to, but I'd kill for Julian.

I sag forward, dropping my head into my hands. "It's Sophie."

"I figured. What happened? Did you guys sleep together?"

"No, worse—at least in her eyes."

He makes a noise. "What's worse?"

Baring her soul and her scars.

I scrub my eyes, remembering hers as she sat across from me at my kitchen table: distant, locked down, guarded. How she'd looked when we met. I'd been so freaking scared she was getting ready to walk out of my life.

She almost did a few times during that convoluted, emotionally charged conversation. I could feel it—a tension like a rubber band pulled taut and about to snap—so I told her about the things Melody said to me. Maybe hoping to save myself. Maybe hoping she *would* leave.

"Are you in love with her?" asks Julian softly.

My head jerks up. "*What?* No. I care about her. She's my friend."

Julian stares at me with so much understanding and patience I almost throw my guitar at him.

Instead, a caustic laugh burns my throat. "*No.*"

He smiles slightly. "I know you remember what I was like after I met Rose. Those months before we finally got together."

He'd been insufferable. Broody as fuck. All over the place. Quick to anger. Easily distracted. *Horrible* to work with in the studio.

"Fuck," I whisper.

He makes a small, sympathetic sound. "Forget the stupid bet with Rose. She doesn't care, anyway. Given her pregnancy brain, she's probably forgotten about it." He pauses, voice softening further. "Unless you don't think Sophie feels the same way?"

"She... she doesn't..." I shake my head, choking on inane laughter. "What the fuck! This is *not* supposed to happen. You can't fall in love when you have a broken heart."

"That's utter bullshit," he says calmly. "The strongest love comes when the heart is a little broken open. It means there's space for deeper roots to grow. And be real, Matt, you and Melody should have never stayed together as long as you did. And you definitely never felt like this"—he points to my twisted face—"about her."

Had I ever lost sleep thinking about Melody before we actually started dating? No, I hadn't. Nor had she rented space in my head twenty-four seven. I'd been drawn to her, sure. I'd enjoyed being around her.

I'd loved her. I *know* I had.

But I hadn't been obsessed with her secrets. Hadn't wanted to touch her so badly it was a physical burn. I'd never woken up every day wishing her head were on the pillow beside mine.

"Sophie…" I cough, and for a second it hits me so hard in the gut I want to fall to my knees and weep. "A few nights ago, she told me why she doesn't do relationships. And I get it. I respect it."

"Huh. I'm guessing the reason isn't something you can share?"

"Definitely not."

Julian sighs. "Friends with benefits is going to blow up in your face if you're already in this deep."

I snort. "Yeah, that's off the table, anyway. She doesn't sleep with people she likes. Casual hookups only for her."

It's rare that Julian is ever at a loss for words, but he opens and closes his mouth a few times. "Shit."

"Exactly."

"What are you going to do?"

I shrug. "The only thing I can do. Be her friend."

Julian winces. "Maybe this whole seeing each other every week thing isn't the best idea."

"She agrees with you. Yesterday, she texted me that we should call it quits. I have no idea when I'm going to see her again." My lips twist sardonically. "But she did say she still wants to be my friend, so there's that."

Julian rubs his forehead. "Jesus."

"I've only known her three months. I've never even kissed her." The words spill from me, thick with confusion and misery. "How is this even happening? Why is she so different?"

Julian's eyes brim with compassion. "Some part of me knew the second I saw Rose. It didn't matter how much I fought it, or how fucked up and complicated things got. I just... knew."

"And all that pain you guys went through?"

I know he understands the question. I know the answer already. But I need to hear it. Even if there's no chance Sophie will ever be mine.

"Worth it."

Now that Sophie has been in my house, I see her everywhere. Especially in the family room, where she tucked herself against me and told me the worst thing I've heard in my life.

She was in the last semester of her three-year art degree and had a showing at a small, local gallery. A wealthy businessman bought four of her drawings and asked for her number. It was an overwhelming, whirlwind romance. He gave her everything she'd thought she'd always wanted. Showered her with expensive gifts, love, physical affection.

Until it changed.

Until he hosted a party at his mansion, predominantly men and scantily dressed women with jaded eyes. Until he slipped drugs into her drink. Until she woke up sore with no memory of the night before. Until it happened again, and again, over the course of six months.

She barely graduated. Lost so much weight her hair started falling out. She started having flashbacks—horrifying flashbacks—and thought she was losing her mind. He gaslit her. Told her it wasn't his fault she drank so much she blacked out every weekend. That maybe she was over-stressed and imagining things. He sent her to get massages and mani-pedis. Bought her diamond earrings.

But the flashbacks grew more frequent and clearer. She might have been painfully naïve, but she wasn't stupid. She finally confronted him, accused him of drugging her and letting his so-called friends rape her.

He went ballistic. Threatened her, her family. Told her she was crazy and no one would believe her. Said she was only good for one thing: making him money.

She lost it and attacked him. They fought. He pulled a gun out of a drawer.

She ran.

With only the clothes on her back, she fled to Josh's apartment. Barely left the bed in his guest room for weeks.

Took a bath one night with a razor and almost didn't see the next day.

Josh found her. Called 911.

The following weeks were a blur. Medications and group therapy. Her mother sobbing. Josh hovering, taking care of her every need, driving her to appointments, spoon-feeding her when she couldn't muster the energy to eat.

Slowly, she clawed her way out of abyss in her mind. Thanks to the therapy groups, she learned she'd been targeted for her youth and innocence. Groomed, manipulated, and victimized. Trafficked by the man who said he loved her.

It was a miracle she got out alive.

Josh took her back to the house a few months later. They found it empty, no evidence of the man or their life together. All traces of him had been wiped from social media, too. She had no pictures, since she'd fled without the phone he'd bought her.

He'd vanished like smoke. A professional predator.

"I realize, on some level, that I'm still letting him control me. But there's a part of me that will always be broken because of what happened. I believed in love and it almost killed me. I don't think I'll never be able to trust my own heart again."

She let me hold her, after. For just a few minutes, her body vibrating and tense against mine. Then she pulled away, wiped the tears from her face, and told me she needed to leave. Needed to see Josh and apologize for their fight.

"Don't cry for me, Matthew," she whispered, those luminous green eyes on my wet face. "I survived. Thousands of women don't."

I let her go. Watched her walk away.

And spent the rest of the night wishing I could have convinced her to stay.

WHEN I GET HOME from Julian's, I go straight to the couch and sit in the same spot we occupied that night. I pull a throw pillow to my side and hug it—a poor substitute for her.

Eventually, I pull out my phone and text her.

> Good night, Dollface

She doesn't reply, just like she hasn't for the last week.

But it's okay.

Sooner or later, she'll realize I'm not going anywhere.

16

"*Did* you see this?" asks Kelly, waving her phone at me from my couch. "Breaking Giants is playing a Halloween show tonight at the Cathedral! Why are we not going?"

I scroll through movies on the television. "Because all the freaks are out tonight. Plus, it's a sold out show."

Kelly's eyes narrow. "You have tickets, though, don't you?"

I wince, lowering the remote. "Maybe," I admit.

There are two tickets at Will Call under my name. Matt texted me yesterday to let me know, but I never responded. I haven't seen him in almost two weeks, since that night at his house. The one time I answered my phone when he called, our conversation was so freaking awkward it took me an hour to stop sweating.

I keep waiting for the day he doesn't text or leave me a voicemail, but it hasn't happened yet.

Kelly drops onto the couch beside me. "Babe, you know I will happily sit here for our annual scary movie marathon. But you can't avoid him forever. Either you want to be friends with him or not."

I knuckle my eyes. "I know. I honestly don't know why I'm fighting it so much. He didn't run away screaming when I told him. He *cried*, for fuck's sake."

"He cares about you, Soph."

"I wish..." I trail off, sighing. "I wish I weren't the way I am. I wish I could break this wall inside me. I care about him, too. I miss him. He makes me laugh. Makes me feel safe."

Kelly wraps an arm around my shoulders and squeezes. "I get that you're afraid. I get that it's complicated." She pauses. "How would you feel, right now, if you found out Matt was seeing someone? Dating a woman who wasn't you?"

I jerk a little. "I—"

"Be honest," she growls.

"I'd hate it," I whisper.

"That's what I thought. So what are you going to do about it? Keep ignoring him until he finally gives up? Or take a leap into the unknown?"

I groan. "Definitely not ready for *that*. And after last

week, I don't even know if he still wants to be friends. Why would he?" The words taste stale. False.

Kelly can hear it, too, and she scoffs. "Now that is some old mental wiring that needs to be ripped out. I don't know Matt well, but I know enough. He's not that guy, Soph. Has he ever shown you that he isn't who he seems to be?"

"No," I murmur.

She jumps to her feet. "Then what the fuck are we doing here? Let's go watch a bunch of hot rock stars do their thing. Wait—are the tickets VIP? Do we get to go backstage?"

The excitement in her voice makes me smile. "Duh."

She squeals and drags me into my bedroom to change. After rejecting the third tiny dress she throws at me, we compromise and I end up in the same black dress Matt told me not to wear to Nick's house.

Kelly rarely dresses down, even for movie nights, so she's set in a dark purple dress and tights with boots. I still eye her with suspicion as I swipe on mascara and some cream blush. Her makeup is already perfect.

"You were going to drag me out tonight either way, weren't you?"

She just cackles.

～

THE CATHEDRAL IS fives times the size of the Lotus Lounge, with a capacity of six hundred, and the marque over the wide entrance says SOLD OUT beneath the band's name. Thanks to Kelly, I now know their Halloween charity show is a longstanding tradition. They've only missed it twice in ten years, and only because they were on tour overseas. The proceeds for the event go to various youth services organizations in the city.

The energy and excitement are palpable, buzzing in my throat as we join the Will Call line. It moves quickly, and once at the window, I give the staff member my name. She checks a list, then reaches behind her for two lanyards with bright orange badges. They're the only two in that color, and Kelly and I trade a look. Apparently, not everyone is as clueless as us, though, because the people behind us start whispering, asking each other who we are.

Then I take the lanyard and lift the badge, seeing the laminated words: *Family All-Access*.

The woman behind the glass—dressed in red with a devil horn headband—smiles and instructs us to head straight to the front of the line. Thankfully, it isn't very long, so we don't feel like elitist assholes. The show is well underway inside, music from the opening act thrumming against our eardrums.

"This is fucking surreal," whisper-shouts Kelly, her arm like a python wrapped around mine.

"No kidding!"

A staff member waves us in, then points toward a roped-off doorway off to the side of the foyer with **Restricted** painted in cursive on the wall beside it. We weave through the crowded space, giant open doors to our left giving us a glimpse of the dark ballroom and distant stage lit up with lights.

The current song ends, the lights dimming, and the crowd roars in approval. "Thank you, Seattle!" shouts the female lead singer. "Good night!"

At the rope, a woman with a headset glances at our lanyards, smiles, and drops the barrier. As we pass, she speaks loudly over the still-screaming crowd. "Up the stairs, down the hallway for a bit, then turn right into another hallway. Greenroom will be on your right." She glances at her watch. "You'll have a few minutes to say hello."

We thank her and tromp up the short flight of stairs, then head down a shadowed hallway. Several people in all black pass us, giving us nods. Voices and a burst of laughter float down the hallway, their origin as yet unseen.

My heart drums in my chest, and my feet are sweating in my combat boots.

"You know I don't get nervous," Kelly says, her voice uncharacteristically tense. "It's just not how I roll. But I'm tripping right now. I feel like I'm going to pee my pants."

My laugh is weak. "Same."

"We should have worn costumes. Did you see how many people are dressed up? I wonder if the band dressed up. Oh my God, I'm gonna vomit."

I pull her to a stop. "We can leave right now, Kel."

Her eyes widen. "What! Shut your mouth." She tugs me forward again. "We're fearless. We belong here. Come on."

I can't help but laugh, and I'm still smiling when we turn the corner and see Nick and Kat standing outside what must be the Greenroom.

"I guess that answers my question," whispers Kelly.

Nick is wearing a unicorn onesie.

Kat, dressed in a matching onesie, sees us and grins. "Hey, ladies!" Then she turns her head and calls loudly, "Matt, Sophie's here!"

Kelly's grip tightens as my knees weaken. She presses close, whispering into my ear, "Breathe."

Matt walks out of the Greenroom, his head swiveling. Kelly makes a choking sound and I can't help it—I start giggling, then slap a hand over my mouth.

He's wearing fringed chaps over blue jeans. No shirt.

A cowboy hat sits askew on his head. I can't even focus on the mouthwatering sight of his bare chest because he looks so ridiculous.

His eyes find me, and his wide grin lights up my body. "This is Rose's fault. Julian's a cowboy, too."

Nick rumbles, "At least he gets to keep his shirt."

Matt takes a few steps toward me, then stops. He glances at Kelly. "Hey. Good to see you."

"Good to be here," she chirps.

Matt looks back at me, his gaze dropping, heating as he notices what I'm wearing. He opens his mouth, but then a stocky, middle-aged man comes out of the Greenroom.

"All right, kids," says who I'm guessing is their manager, Phil. "Time to boogie."

Julian, Rose, Jackson, and a few others I don't recognize flood the hallway, forcing Matt closer. I barely manage to return waves from Rose and Julian. Matt's too close—too *everything*. I suck in a breath and his scent floods my nose. Kelly slips away from me.

"It's really good to see you," he says, scanning my face.

"Same." My voice cracks. Heat floods my cheeks, which makes Matt's lips tilt up. "Thanks for inviting me."

He touches a knuckle to the badge hanging from my

neck. Despite the lack of actual contact, I feel the vibration in my bones.

"My friends are my family," he says softly, "and you're my friend."

"Matt!" hollers Jackson from the end of the hallway.

He waves over his shoulder, never breaking eye contact. "Will you hang for a bit after the set?"

I nod dumbly.

He grins. "I like the pigtails. And I love that dress. See you after, Dollface."

He turns and jogs down the rapidly emptying hallway. My eyes drink in the sight of my art on his tattooed back, the design from shoulders to waist complete. Perfect.

"Whew! I could light a match from the heat between you two." Kelly sidles up to me and hands me a pair of slim, bright yellow earplugs, then a sealed bottle of water. "Kat gave me these and told me where to go. Are you ready? Or are you going to stand here drooling for the next two hours?"

I sputter. She smiles sweetly, then reclaims my arm and leads me down the hallway.

17

Of course our position offstage would be the closest to Matt. *Of course.* He's ten feet away, glistening with sweat. He lost the hat partway through the first song, throwing it into the crowd—much to their delight.

As the set progresses, there comes a point when I can barely look at him anymore because every glimpse cranks my need up another level. His lips on the mic as he harmonizes with Julian. The way stage lights dance over his face. Muscles bunching, body twisting as he performs. The electric energy he exudes, that weaves seamlessly with his other band members. Even the sweat dripping down his back and darkening the waist of his jeans is fucking torture.

Halfway through the ninety-minute set, Rose moves

beside me and bumps her shoulder to mine. Surprisingly, I don't flinch. Maybe it's the visible curve of her stomach or the beatific smile on her face, but I smile back.

When the song—one of their early hits—ends, the crowd goes berserk. A woman sitting on someone's shoulders yanks her shirt up and screams Julian's name—the name also painted across her bare breasts. Shocked, I glance at Rose, but she only laughs and leans close.

"It's the name of the game," she says, her voice muted but clear through my earplug. "Eventually, you have to decide if it's going to bother you or not. And if it bothers you, you're probably with the wrong person."

I nod like I understand what she's saying and pretend I don't know why she's saying it to me.

Onstage, the men towel themselves off and suck down water. Julian chats with the crowd while a runner darts past us to hand Matt a different guitar. As he's lifting the strap over his head, he glances up—right at me.

He grins and mouths the words, *"Hi, Dollface,"* before focusing on his instrument.

For the next six songs, I'm back to staring at him, like maybe there's an answer in the line of his cheekbones or the grip of his hand on the neck of his guitar.

And almost an hour later, as the stage lights dim after the third encore, I'm still looking for an answer when Kelly, Rose, Kat, and I make a stop in the bathroom, then head back to the Greenroom.

The guys are already inside, sprawled out and visibly exhausted. Julian chugs water, wet hair plastered to his head. Jackson has a towel over his face, the curly blond wig he was wearing discarded on the floor. Nick is groaning and trying to tug off the last leg of his onesie. And Matt sits against the far wall in a folding chair, his legs stretched out, head against the wall, eyes closed.

Rose laughs softly and heads for Julian just as Phil sweeps into the room and bellows, "What are you, a bunch of retirees? Get it together. Press and meet-and-greet start in twenty at the side stage!"

There's a deep, unified groan from the men.

"We're not twenty-five anymore," Nick whines, lifting the leg still trapped in the unicorn costume and waving it at his wife.

"Poor baby," Kat croons, smirking as she helps him free his foot.

Kelly veers toward the table set up with a variety of food and drinks. I glance at Matt—whose eyes are still closed—then join her to snag two beers from their bed of ice. I pop the tops.

"I'm guessing neither of those is for me?" she whispers. I shake my head slowly, and she grins. "Go on, then."

With a steadying breath, I cross the room and sit in the chair beside Matt's.

"God, you smell good," he murmurs. One eye cracks open, then the other, and his head rotates toward me. I force myself to meet his gaze, even though I feel naked beneath it.

"Better than you, that's for sure," I say with a grimace.

A smile teases his lips. "I've missed your sass."

"Because you're unhinged." I hand him a beer; he hums his thanks and downs half of it in one go. "Do you want me to get you some food? There's salad, pizza, sandwiches…"

That damn smile grows. "Nah. If I eat before the meet-and-greet, all I'll think about is taking a nap. How about you? Hungry?"

Define hungry.

I shrug, worrying my nail against the label on my bottle. "Sort of. Not really. I'll just make something when I get home."

"Or you can let me. Make you food, that is."

My gaze flies back to him. "Aren't you exhausted?"

"Physically, yes. But my brain is wired from the show. I'll probably see the sunrise."

There's a question in his eyes that mirrors the one I've been asking for an hour.

And I finally know the answer.

"Okay."

PHIL HERDS the band down the hallway, through a door, and down some stairs into Cathedral's side stage, a smaller venue for lesser known acts. The overhead lights are on, and the place is set up with long tables in a U-shape, where fans who've either purchased or won access browse snacks and free swag.

When the men step onto the floor, they're instantly swarmed. I hang back with Rose and Kat. Kelly spends a few minutes snagging swag, then joins us at the folding chairs set up near the stage.

Before long, Roses's words during the show are ringing in my ears. Women shamelessly plaster themselves against Matt. From girls in their early twenties to women in their fifties, every one of them cops a feel before getting him to sign swag. They ask him for selfies, they ask him if they can kiss his cheek. They fawn and flaunt and simper.

At least he found a T-shirt to put on.

I stiffen as a stunning brunette tucks herself into his

side and smiles up at him. Rose's dark eyes flicker to me, but thankfully Kat distracts her by muttering, "Get your hands away from his ass, bitch."

I glance over and see a woman hugging Nick like he's her long-lost love. And yes, her hands are precariously close to gripping his ass. To Nick's credit, he neatly extricates himself and turns to the next fan.

Rose says idly, "I like to remind myself how nasty they smell right now."

"Right?" Kat shudders. "The ball sweat alone, my God. I guarantee none of these women would be quite so excited to deal with the dirty laundry."

Rose laughs. "I make Julian do it. He's not allowed to use the hamper, either. He has to dump everything straight in the washer."

"Oh, good one. I'm gonna try that."

Beside me, Kelly leans forward to address the women. "How long do these typically last?"

Kat shrugs. "An hour or two. Depends on how badly the guys want to go home." She glances at Rose with a smirk. "Sometimes we'll start sexting our husbands. That usually speeds things up."

We all laugh as she pulls out her phone and waves it at Rose, who shakes her head. "Too soon. Let's give them forty-five minutes."

A half-hour later, Kelly starts listing in her seat and

periodically yawning. Guilt spikes me; she worked an early shift today and it's past midnight.

I bend her way and murmur, "You can head out if you want, Kel. Matt's going to, uh, take me home."

Her eyes sparkle as they widen. "Really?"

I nod with a thousand times more confidence than I feel. "We're going to eat and hang for a while."

My voice is low, but not low enough. Kat declares, "Just make sure he showers first, I'm tellin' ya!"

Kelly laughs as my face heats with embarrassment. "You're not upset?" I ask her.

"Hell no! I'm dead on my feet and was feeling all guilty because I was going to ask you to leave in a minute."

I smile. "Okay. I'll walk you out."

She trades goodbyes with Rose and Kat, and we head toward the entrance. In the foyer, my phone starts buzzing in my pocket.

"Who the hell is calling you at this hour?"

My heart trips, then pounds. I whip out my phone, terrified I'll see my mom's number, then blink a few times when Matt's face pops up. Blowing out a relieved breath, I accept the call and put the phone to my ear.

"Hello?"

"Tell me you didn't just leave."

I chew on my lip, fighting a smile. "I didn't. Just walking Kelly out."

There's a two-second pause. "Give me five minutes and we'll be out of here, too."

The line goes dead.

My mouth open, I look up at Kelly's smug face. She grabs me in a tight hug. "Whatever happens tonight—talking, sexy times, pedicures, whatever—just know how freaking proud I am of you. You are the baddest bitch I know."

My heart starts racing, for a different reason this time. "Thanks, Kel," I whisper.

18

To my surprise, there's little fanfare as Matt and I slip out the back of the venue to the parking lot. There's a small crowd of fans, maybe fifteen people, corralled behind a cement divide by one of the venue's staff. I linger in the background as Matt chats for a few minutes and takes photos. Then we're in his car and driving out of downtown.

At a stoplight, he pulls open the neck of his shirt and sniffs. "Sorry about the stench. Do you care if I shower when we get home? I mean... you know what I mean. To my house. Or do you need to stop at home? Your place, I mean?"

"I'm good," I say calmly, even though I'm laughing inside. I throw his words from weeks ago back at him. "You're nervous."

"Damn straight," he says, throwing me a grin that sparks a flare in my belly. "How are you? What have you been up to?"

I roll my eyes. "Haven't you figured out by now that I don't have an exciting life? Any given week, I work, sleep, draw, repeat."

"I like your life. And I like being in your life. Thanks for hanging out with me." He pauses, and I'm grateful for the darkness disguising my face. "Whenever you want to leave, I can drive you home or get you an Uber. Whatever you want."

"Matthew, stop babying me."

His lips curve. "Sorry-not-sorry. So, how'd you like the show?"

"You guys are amazing. No surprise there."

"Is that the first time you've seen us live?"

I nod. "I know it'll come as a shock, but I don't go to a lot of concerts."

He grins. "Except with me, because I get you the good seats."

I laugh. "Yes."

We lapse into companionable silence for the rest of the drive. When he pulls into his driveway, I'm still surprisingly calm. Even his self-proclaimed stench doesn't bother me; it's just *him*, amplified by sweat. It comforts me the same way his clean smell does.

He hits a button, and the single-car garage door rolls up. He pulls inside, turns off the car, and the big door hums closed.

"What are you feeling?" he asks as we walk inside the house. "Something fast like grilled cheese? How hungry are you?"

So fucking hungry, but not for food.

I take off my coat and hang it on a peg near the garage door. "Grilled cheese sounds perfect. But I can wait for you to shower."

"Okay." He smiles over his shoulder. "Feel free to snack on whatever you find in the fridge. I think there's some leftover pasta salad."

I shoo him away. "Go, go."

For the next fifteen minutes, I sit curled up in a corner of his living room couch under a blanket that smells like him. I take out my French braids and finger comb through the loose strands, sighing at the relief in my scalp. I scroll on my phone for a few minutes, and finally, I hear his footsteps in the hallway.

I throw the blanket aside. Sit up and cross my legs. Then uncross them. I debate running to the bathroom to check my hair and makeup, but the moment I finally decide to do it, he strides into the room. I freeze halfway off the couch.

He's in sweatpants, a soft T-shirt, and beat-up house

slippers, his hair damp and face flushed from the shower. And all I can think is, *Is he wearing underwear?*

"What are you doing, Dollface?" he asks lightly.

"Nothing."

Eyes narrowing even as his smile widens, he glances pointedly around the room. "Did you find anything interesting? I kind of expected every drawer and cabinet to be open by now."

"Pfft."

He chuckles. "Did you at least get something to drink or a snack?" Before I can answer, he shakes his head. "Never mind. I know you didn't. Come on, keep me company in the kitchen. Do you, uh, want to change?" he asks without looking at me. "Unless you're comfortable—"

"I'm fine, thanks."

I ignore the probing look he sends my way, slipping onto a stool at the marble island. After depositing a beer, a glass of ice water, and a small bowl of mixed nuts on the surface before me, he starts pulling items from the fridge and cabinets.

I sip and nibble and watch him move with the same easy confidence with which he does everything. He doesn't ignore me, either, keeping a light conversation flowing. He asks what my favorite Halloween costume was as a kid, if my mom gets a lot of Trick or Treaters, and whether I did the expected "Fall Pumpkin Farm Trip" this year. He lets it slip that pumpkin hunting and carving had been one of his friend-date ideas for us.

"I'm sorry," I say haltingly, my body warm from the beer on a mostly empty stomach. I take a quick sip of water. "For ignoring you the last couple weeks."

A soft smile flashes toward me as he sets a plate down, piled high with slices of grilled cheese, then settles on the stool beside mine.

"You're forgiven," he says. "Let's eat."

The grilled cheese is excellent, on thick, perfectly toasted sourdough with three different kinds of cheese and ribbons of fresh basil. We wash it down with fresh beers.

"So good. Thank you," I mumble around my final bite.

"You're welcome. Do you feel like watching a movie? Or are you sick of me yet?"

"So sick of you," I deadpan, then grab the plate and head for the sink.

"You don't have to—"

"Shut up, Matt."

He chuckles. "Fine. I'll be on the couch."

I clean up the kitchen, which is barely messy since he's one of those freaks who clean as they cook, then wander into the living room. Matt sits in the center of the couch, flipping through Halloween movie offerings on the television.

I settle beside him, careful to keep a foot of space between us. His scent still wraps around me. Clean skin and that indefinable musk—*pheromones*, I acknowledge—that make my blood simmer.

"Didn't you tell me you usually do a movie marathon for Halloween?"

The casual words inexplicably make the pressure between my legs *worse*. Maybe it's the evidence he listens. That he cares about and retains random shit I've told him over the weeks. I think I mentioned the Halloween tradition last month.

I screw my eyes shut.

"Sophie?" His voice is concerned. Alarmingly close. The heat from his body radiates onto my side. "What's wrong?"

The first thing I see when I open my eyes is his mouth, and I move without much conscious effort. Like a flower seeking sunlight, I know only that he has what I need to survive.

He freezes as my lips graze his. I jerk back, mortified, but the look on his face stops me.

"Do it again," he whispers. "Please."

With a sigh, I fit my mouth against his. Slowly, I learn the contours I've daydreamed about for so long.

His lips are warm and soft. *So soft.* He kisses me back gently, following my lead. After a few more seconds pass without much passion on his end, doubt stirs in my mind. Does he not want this? Or is he just being respectful?

"You can touch me," I say against his lips.

His hands settle on my waist, hot and strong, fingers like brands through the material of my dress. Relief fades swiftly, though, when they don't move and the kiss doesn't deepen.

Embarrassment floods me anew and I lean back. I'm horrified when my eyes start burning. I touch my lips, shaking my head. "I'm sorry, I—"

"No," he says quickly. "Shit. Sophie, look at me."

I do, though maintaining eye contact ranks as one of the hardest things I've ever done. Everything in me wants to sprint out the front door and never look back.

"I want you," he says, voice hoarse. "So fucking much. I'm trying not to…" He swallows hard, eyes closing. His hands leave my waist, which feels suddenly cold. "Fuck."

I scoot back on the couch. Even though it's never happened before—I've never slept with someone who knows the truth of my past—there's no misreading this. It's everything I was afraid of. An emotional car crash in slow motion.

"You think I'm broken." My voice is toneless, almost cold. I stand up, hugging my arms to my chest. "I knew this would happen. I'm so fucking stupid."

He jerks to standing. "Don't put words in my mouth. That's not what's happening."

"What is it, then?" The ice inside me cracks; darkness floods my voice. "Is it disgust? You don't want what a bunch of men have already had?"

His face whitens. "*What?* No." His hands clench and unclench at his sides. "Can we take a breath? You're not some casual hookup to me. I care about you. And I'm not an idiot. I know there's a huge chance if we do this, you'll run."

"I..." I trail off, unable to lie and equally incapable of admitting the truth.

He nods curtly. "Exactly. You're blowing up the boundaries of our friendship right now, and I still mean what I said—I want you in my life more than I want you in my bed."

A pained noise escapes me. I can't even look at him. "You're friend-zoning me?"

When he's quiet, my gaze lifts to his face. He doesn't look happy, but I can't read his expression. "What do you want from me?" he asks softly. "Tell me it's more than one night."

I shake my head. "Honestly, I hadn't thought that far

ahead. I don't know why it has to be that complicated. Do you want me or not?"

He laughs shortly, sharp and without humor. "I'm trying not to make a giant mistake. Don't you get it? I'm already half in love with you, Sophie. Can you say the same? Do you care about me at all as more than a friend or a random hookup? Because my heart can't fucking take another hit right now."

My head, my body, *everything* reels from his words. "What?" I whisper.

He snorts. "Don't pretend you're surprised."

I shake my head mutely. I *am* surprised. Floored. My thoughts are a jumbled mess. My heart feels like it's seconds from splintering into a million pieces.

"You don't mean that," I blurt. "You can't be. I'm not..."

"Not what?" he demands. "Not the most beautiful woman I've ever seen? The most fascinating, talented, funny, smart, sexy, *perfect* woman?" He throws his hands up. "I feel like the universe is playing a sick joke on me. 'Hey, Matt, I know your fiancée just bailed, so here's your dream woman, but she's completely emotionally unavailable. Good luck, buddy!'"

I listen numbly to his tirade, my heart drumming in my ears. An image takes shape in my mind: two giant waves full of broken debris heading straight for each other.

"You're not falling in love with me, Matt." My voice is soft but firm. "I'm just the first person to come along. You latched onto me because my art is on your back, because you were brokenhearted and needed a distraction."

"Really?" he barks. "That's what you think?"

The waves in my mind make contact, slamming together in a mass of churning whitewater and sharp objects.

"If you actually wanted me, you would have kissed me like you fucking meant—"

He's on me as the last word passes my lips, his hot, furious mouth claiming the final consonant. One arm brackets my lower back, sealing our bodies together, while his other hand captures the base of my neck.

"Like this?" he growls against my lips.

I gasp, and his tongue takes advantage, diving in to brand mine. My legs go weak. As I sag in his arms, he sits on the couch, forcing me to straddle him. Never breaking the seal of our mouths, he pulls up the hem of my dress, hot fingers branding the bare skin of my thighs before grabbing my ass and yanking my hips forward. His own hips rise, his thick erection sliding against the lace over my throbbing center.

I whimper as he finds a devastating rhythm, his tongue and hips driving me fast toward a glimmering edge. His arms hold me close, forcing friction my body is all too willing to exploit.

I plummet over that glowing boundary, whimpering and jerking as the orgasm rocks through me. My body clamps down on nothing, weeping for him. His hand dives around the back of my thigh, sneaking beneath my underwear to stroke along my tender, soaking center.

"Fuck," he groans.

I grab his lower lip in my teeth. He grunts and bites me back, then sucks my tongue into his mouth. My hands dive between us, scrambling for the waist of his sweatpants.

"Sophie, no," he whispers.

I barely hear him; that is, until he captures my hands and lifts them between us. Panting, I stare at him dumbly.

"What do you mean, no?"

He's so fucking gorgeous. Flushed cheekbones, swollen lips, soft, gray-blue eyes. "We're not going any further tonight."

My eyes narrow. Something sharp flies toward the fragile surface of my post-orgasm glow. "Why not?" I shift a little in his lap and am rewarded by a hiss of breath through his teeth.

"Because as amazing as it would be to bury myself inside you and fuck you until neither of us can walk, we're going to cuddle instead."

The visual makes me burn, then his final words register. "I'm sorry, *what*? Is this you trying to win that stupid—"

"It's not about the bet. I don't care about that anymore, and according to Julian, Rose already forgot about it. It was dumb, anyway—just an excuse to make you agree to be my friend without feeling like I was pressuring you into more."

"Then why?" I tug my dress down, which is impossible while straddling him, so I scramble off his lap and yank the fabric over my knees. With a pointed glance at what's tenting his sweatpants, I repeat, "Why?"

His gaze lifts from my legs. "Because if you touch me, it's all over. Maybe I've lost my mind? I don't know. I've already told you I'm falling for you, so maybe this is me trying to protect myself a little longer."

My lungs squeeze. *He can't possibly mean that.*

"Matt..."

He jumps up, wincing as he adjusts himself. "I know, I know. This is a disaster in the making. But I don't want you to go yet. Will you stay the night? Will Pickle be okay? I can set an alarm and drive you home in the morning. Do you work tomorrow?"

"Pickle's fine," I say softly. "He's used to me sleeping late. As long as I'm home by ten to feed him. And yes, I work at one."

"Okay." He pauses. "Does this mean you'll stay?"

I shouldn't. I really, really shouldn't.

But I'm lost at sea.

"Yes, I'll stay."

19

When I wake up, it takes me a minute to realize I'm not dreaming. There's a thick, tattooed arm around my waist, and a giant Viking cuddling me. It's the same as—and so, so different from—six years ago. For one, he's still wearing sweatpants, and I'm wearing one of his T-shirts over my underwear. His hips aren't pressed against me, but he's still a furnace against my spine, his breath stirring the hair on the top of my head.

I feel... safe.

I never, ever want to get up.

But the longer I lie in his arms, the more my brain turns on and the more scared I become. Not physically. *Worse.* Because as much as I denied it last night, the new day mocks me with the clarity of my thoughts. The waves have settled and the sun blazes down like truth serum, shining on all the wreckage floating on the surface of the water.

This isn't casual—for either of us. But whereas Matt seems ready to go all in, to explore the bond between us like a reasonably sane, emotionally mature adult...

I'm not.

And it's not that I don't want to. I want to so badly that tears spring to my eyes even thinking about it. But the darkness inside me doesn't care about what my heart wants.

That darkness—I've learned all it wants is to protect me from pain. It's the remains of myself at twenty: the sheltered girl who was swept off her feet by a charming smile and flashing eyes and all the trappings of wealth.

I hate her. Pity her. Sometimes, I mourn her. But I don't know if I'll ever forgive her.

Matt mumbles but stays asleep as I slip from the bed and find my dress, socks, and shoes. I take everything and go downstairs, dressing swiftly in the hallway bathroom.

Then I call an Uber and do exactly what he said I'd do.

I run.

~

"Go home, Sophie."

Allison leans in the doorway of my office, a sympathetic smile on her lips.

"I'm fine," I say, pushing hair from my face and sitting up straight. "Just a late night."

"Whatever you say," she says softly, "but I still want you to go home. I already talked to Brian and he's cool with closing. Dania will be here to help him before I leave for the day."

I rub my face. "Am I that out of it?"

"You've been staring at your dark computer screen for a half hour." She takes a step into the office. "Anything you want to talk about?"

I open my mouth to say no, but what comes out instead is, "I don't know how to date someone. You know, be in a relationship."

In two seconds flat, Allison occupies the chair opposite my desk, her dark gaze avid on my face. "Is this about who I think it's about?"

I drop my head into my arms. "Yeah."

There's a long pause. "I'd be scared, too."

My head whips up. "What?"

She nods solemnly. "Matt comes with a lot of baggage. Or maybe that's the wrong word. Complications? The main one being he's famous, and, well... even I can admit that he's smoking hot. Random musicians don't normally pose half-naked on the cover of GQ, ya know?"

I flush, nodding. I remember the cover and inside spread well. *Too well.* I still have a copy of the four-year-old magazine in my closet—which I should probably get rid of immediately.

Allison continues, "The thing is, now that Julian's off the market, and Matt's technically back *on* it, he's the center of the fandom's attention." She shudders. "Never read comments under Matt's photos on the band's Instagram. They'll make you worry for the future of womankind."

"This isn't really helping," I mutter.

She winces. "I know, sorry. I've always liked Matt, though. Despite his reputation—and the inevitable collection of resentful women he's dumped—he doesn't act like a dirtbag who thinks he's God's gift to vaginas. He's a one-woman-at-a-time guy. Plus, from what Rose has told me about the shit that went down with his ex, I guess he was way more invested than she was." She shrugs. "My long-winded point is that maybe Matt doesn't know how to do relationships, either."

"*Definitely* not helping."

"What I'm trying to say is that none of us really know what we're doing. We all have our hangups and fears. I was cheated on in my last relationship, and every day I have to stop myself from snooping in Katie's phone. I have a totally irrational belief she's going to hurt me the same way."

I sigh sadly. "I'm sorry, Allison."

There's a long pause, then she says gently, "Something bad happened to you." When my eyes narrow, she lifts a hand. "I know the signs. My stepsister, Iris, has PTSD from something that happened to her when she was young. She struggles with trusting men, too, and relationships are a challenge. I'm not asking you to tell me anything. I just want you to know that there's nothing wrong with you. You're doing your best, Soph, and your best is *always* enough."

I shake my head. "I wish it felt that way. I've spent years convincing myself that I'm happy alone and now... now I don't know how to change. For the first time, I kind of want to." I swallow hard and rub my aching eyes. "And you're right—something bad did happen. Almost ten years ago. Even though all this time has passed, it's like that experience warped something inside me. I know Matt would never hurt me like that. But there's a wall inside me between knowing and believing it."

Allison sits forward, eyes simmering with compassion. "You know what I call people without trauma?"

"What?"

"Boring."

A tired smile tugs my mouth. "Ha."

"I'm sorry for whatever happened to you. I wish I had some advice. All I can tell you is that you're an awesome person, Sophie, and I'm not surprised at all that you've caught the eye of someone like Matt. No matter what happens with you guys, I hope he's worthy of you."

"Thanks, Allison," I whisper.

She smiles back and stands. "Now pack your shit. Go home. Listen to loud music and make some art."

As she's turning to leave, a part-timer, Candace, pops her head into the office. She looks nervous, eyes darting between us. "Hey, bosses. What am I supposed to do when someone comes in and starts asking us questions about one of you? I mean, we obviously said nothing, but now they're bugging customers." She's looking right at me, leaving no doubt which one of us she's referring to.

I frown and stand. "What the hell? What are they saying?"

Allison sighs and tells her, "I'll handle it."

After giving me a wide-eyed glance filled with curiosity, Candace leaves.

A bad feeling grows legs in my belly as I round the desk. "Allison?" I ask, somewhat shrilly.

She pulls out her phone, saying distractedly, "Hang on. Ah, here it is." She winces and passes me her phone.

The first thing I see is a weeks-old photo of Matt and me inside Lotus Lounge. We're standing at the bar, his arms bracketing me. I'm looking up at him. He's staring at my mouth.

Mystery Woman Responsible For Matt Sullivan's Split from Fiancé?

Cold radiates down my arms.

"Don't panic," Allison says, grabbing the phone before I can read the short article. "And don't worry. I'm well versed in this particular shitshow after the Rose-Julian debacle three years ago."

I stare at her. "If someone is here, it means they know who I am."

"Everyone's a private detective these days," she says, waving a hand dismissively. "You head out the back. I'll brief the staff on how we handle the press. And whatever you do, don't read the stupid article."

I wait until I get to my car before pulling out my phone and searching for the article. It's really more of a blurb, with a link to an Instagram account full of trashy celebrity photos and gossip. There, a few rows down, I find the image of Matt and me. It's a slideshow, and I swipe through three more photos of us from that night.

The last photo is the most damning, at least in my eyes. It's the moment he caught me in his arms. My scalp prickles as I think about that violent shove. Was it intentional? Were there two people working together? The photo is overtly suggestive; it looks like I'm purposely splayed against him. Instead of the reality— him catching me so I didn't fall—it looks like he's very much a willing participant.

My fingers shake as I scroll down and expand the caption beneath the photos, which is just a repeat of what was on the webpage.

Spotted! Breaking Giants' Matt Sullivan with mystery woman at Lotus Lounge.

Could she be the reason for the recent split between Matt and his fiancée, Melody Finnegan? Fans are disappointed and demanding an explanation!

"Fucking assholes," I mutter, throwing my phone into my purse.

I make the short drive home, vowing to ignore the poisonous impulse inside me to fall down the Google rabbit hole. Are there other pictures out there? What are people saying about me?

None of my business, I remind myself as I lock my car and trudge up the stairs to my apartment.

"Stupid," I mutter. "She told you not to read it."

Clearing the final flight of stairs—and wishing I'd taken the elevator—I round the corner into my hallway with the intention of face-planting on my couch as soon as possible.

I jerk to a stop at the sight of the man sitting against my front door. His blond head is bowed, arms resting on his bent knees.

He looks up. "Hi, Dollface."

20

"You knew I was working today. Did you forget? Or were you seriously going to wait here until I got off? That's insane. Anyone could have seen you. Why didn't you just call me?" My voice—like my brain—is unhinged.

Matt crosses my apartment and sinks onto the couch. "I don't know." His voice is subdued, his gaze not meeting mine for more than a second or two. "I wasn't really thinking, I guess. Then I heard Pickle inside, so I ended up sitting down. We were having deep conversations through the door."

The cat in question jumps onto the couch and curls up next to Matt's jean-clad thigh. His golden feline eyes stare at me for a few seconds before he headbutts Matt, who obliges his clear demand for scritches. In seconds, Pickle is purring, his eyes half-closed.

I pour myself a glass of water and drink it in a few long gulps, trying to slow down my racing heart.

"Did you see the photos? Online?"

Matt looks up, frowning. "What photos?"

I set my glass down. "Of us at Lotus Lounge. The article implies I broke you and your ex up."

His brows lift. "I don't read that crap or use social media. You shouldn't, either."

I blink. "You... never? Not even Instagram?"

He shakes his head. "We have people who manage all our profiles. I think Nick and Jackson have private accounts for family and stuff, but Julian and I don't. It's a toxic wasteland."

"Oh."

A smile flirts with his mouth. "Oh?"

I clear my throat. "So I shouldn't worry that someone figured out where I work and came into Tullamore today to harass my employees?"

He sits up, eyes narrowing. Pickle meeps and jumps to the floor. "What? Shit." He drags his hands through his hair. "This is my fault. I should have expected something like this, or at least warned you it could happen."

"Matt?"

He looks up, concerned eyes finding mine. "Yeah?"

"It's okay." Surprisingly, I mean it. His words, his voice, his presence—whatever the secret, magical mix is, I feel calm again. "I won't pay attention to anything I see online."

"Really?"

He looks so shocked, I smile. "Yes, really. It caught me off guard today, but it's not your fault. You're famous, super approachable, and nice to your fans. It was bound to happen eventually if we kept hanging out in public."

I cross to the couch and sit beside him, picking up the remote and turning on the TV. Matt shifts on the couch so he's facing me, his heavy stare probing the side of my face. After a few seconds of trying to ignore it, I sigh and turn to him.

"Do I like being slandered? No. But you're right, social media is toxic as fuck. And at the end of the day, the same rules apply online as in life. It's none of my business what people say or think about me. It only matters what I think. What you think."

"I think you're amazing," he says quietly.

Flushing, I fiddle with the remote. "Yeah, you're not so bad yourself."

"You snuck out this morning." There's no accusation in his tone, just a muted hurt that makes me think of him sitting hunched against my front door.

My heart squeezes, and my eyes close. "I'm trying," I

whisper. "I want to try." Forcing myself to look at him, I add, "Is that going to be enough?"

"Yes," he murmurs, eyes scanning my face. "I'll take whatever you want to give me, Sophie Marshall."

My pulse ramps up. "And if I want to give you a kiss?"

His lips part on a swift breath, his features tightening, eyes darkening. Anticipation zings down my body, settling into a pulse between my legs.

"Come here," he whispers. "Right now."

I move forward. He catches my knee and draws it over his lap. I settle on his thighs, my hands lifting to frame his face. I trace his features with my greedy fingers, absorbing everything: his warm skin, dark gold brows, the slight roughness along his jaw, the curve of his cheekbones, the outline of his lips. I drink in the sight and feel of him as tension crackles between us.

"Sophie," he breathes.

Leaning forward, I press my lips to his. It's nothing like the first time. Or even the second. Instead, it's somewhere in the soft space between restraint and abandon. He lets me set the pace, but there's no question of his investment. Especially when I lick the seam of his lips and he opens for me with a low groan.

I press closer, angling my head for a deeper kiss. I'm lost in him. Breathing underwater. His arms band around my back, tight and secure. I don't feel constricted, though. I feel treasured.

"Matt?" I whisper, panting as I lift my head. He drops velvet-soft kisses along my jaw, down my neck, and back up to my ear.

He nips my earlobe. "Yes, Sophie?"

"Take me to bed."

He stills, vibrating with focus, breath hot on my ear. "Only if you ask nicely and you don't kick me out right after."

My pulse skyrockets. "Deal. Now *please* take me to bed."

I yelp as he rockets off the couch with me in his arms, one arm braced beneath my ass, my legs dangling. Figuring he can find the bedroom easily enough, I devote myself to learning the contours of his throat with my lips and tongue.

The light around us dims as he enters my bedroom, the blackout drapes mostly closed. There's enough light to see, though, and he wastes no time lowering me onto my comforter. I sigh at the glorious pressure of his weight atop me and grab the hem of his long-sleeved shirt, yanking it up. He lifts his arms to help, and I throw the fabric to the floor.

"Goddamn," I whisper in pure female satisfaction,

running my hands greedily over his cut torso, my nails tracing lines of ink and muscle.

"Your turn," he growls, and my shirt sails across the room a moment later. On his knees, he stares down at my bra-clad chest. I squirm under the attention and gasp as his fingers trail up my abdomen and between my breasts, skirting the lines of various tattoos and enflaming every inch of my skin. "Too fucking beautiful."

His head dips. I arch up, gasping as his hot mouth closes over the peak of one breast, soaking the thin material of my bra. He lavishes the same attention on my other breast before undoing the clasp between the cups and tossing the material aside. My nipples, already tight, tingle at the touch of cool air.

Matt stares down at me, unmoving, his jaw clenched. I squirm. "What is it?"

"You have no idea how many times I've imagined this," he murmurs, "but it's even better in reality." He palms my breasts, teasing my nipples first with his fingers, then with his mouth.

Half-insane with need, I manage to unbutton his jeans and lower the zipper. He grunts as I curl my fingers around the erection straining the fabric of his boxer briefs. *Holy shit, he's big.* I knew he was, but there's a major difference between visualizing and actually touching the evidence.

He thrusts into my hand as he licks and kisses his way back to my mouth. "I'm on birth control," I mumble into his lips, "and the condoms I have won't fit you."

His head jerks up, eyes brimming with shock and laughter. "I'm... flattered. I don't have any, either, but I'm not worried. There are a thousand things we can do with each other that don't require a condom."

"No way," I say with a pointed squeeze of my hands. He shudders, his eyes going hazy. "I want this. I've wanted it for years. And I trust you."

His gaze softens. "I trust you, too."

"Then it's settled. Take off your pants, Matthew."

He kisses me hard, then rolls off the bed, standing to kick off his shoes and pull off his pants. The sight of him in all his naked glory is so distracting that my jeans are barely over my hips by the time he crawls back onto the bed.

"Let me."

He slides the denim down my legs, pulling my underwear with it. On his way back up my body, he stalls halfway, pushing my legs up and lowering his head.

"Matt—" The rest of the words knot in my throat as his mouth closes over me. I grip his soft hair as he sucks and licks me ravenously, humming his enjoyment until I'm writhing against his face, close to falling off the edge.

Then he stops.

"Rude," I gasp, lifting my head to glare.

He kisses his way up my belly, a self-satisfied smile on his face. "Patience."

I make a frustrated sound that softens to a sigh as he settles atop me and claims my mouth. His cock drags against my belly, the base teasing my clit. I wriggle shamelessly against him, my body screaming for a release.

"You can ride my face again later," he whispers into my mouth. "But this time..." He notches himself at my entrance, groaning when I tilt my hips and he sinks inside an inch. "This time you're coming on my cock."

I bite my lip and drive my hips upward. We moan together as he sinks in further. My body contracts around him and he hisses. I grab his waist, clenching hot skin, and drive up again. *More, more.* He's not even halfway inside me and I'm already close to coming.

"Fuck, fuck," he chants, forehead dropping to mine. "You feel better than anything. Shit, I'm not going to last long."

I nip at his jaw, then his lower lip, tugging gently at the soft flesh. "Fuck me, Matthew. *Please.*"

He finally relents, sinking inside me fully, tearing a

ragged cry from my throat at the immediate, mind-blowing fullness, the delicious stretch.

"Are you okay?" he whispers, kissing my forehead, my closed eyes.

"Yes, yes," I breathe out. "You feel perfect. So perfect."

"So do you," he growls. "Now hang on to me because I can't be gentle. I want you too much."

Exhilaration fires up my spine as I wrap myself around him, and he makes good on his threat, fucking me like he wants to disappear inside me. His tongue never parts from mine, each kiss a dark promise of what's headed our way. It doesn't take long for that delicious pressure to build inside me again, magnified by the grind of his pelvis on my clit.

"Oh, fuck, Matt, I can't..."

"Let go," he murmurs. "I'll catch you."

My orgasm is a tempest, almost violent in its intensity, a pleasure so unmatched it flirts with pain. I hear his voice in my ear, telling me how perfect I feel, how he can feel me pulsing, squeezing him, how much he's wanted this. Tears leak from my eyes as he swells and grows impossibly hard inside me.

"Sophie," he whispers, "I—" The word is choked off by a guttural groan as he stiffens and joins me inside the storm.

aylight is waning, just a hint of gray light outside, but the candle on the dresser is enough for me to see every inch of her bare back. Every tattooed inch. I've been staring at her for a good half-hour while she sleeps, her hair tangled on the pillow, a sheet draped low on her hips. I can't stop staring.

It's *my* tattoo.

Adapted for her smaller, thinner frame, it's a feminine version of *my freaking* tattoo. And on the wall next to her closet are the original drawings, side by side.

I remind myself she had no idea who Josh tattooed her artwork on, but it doesn't help the chain reaction happening in my heart. I'm not even surprised, honestly. Of course we'd have giant, complementary tattoos. Of course.

Because she's it.

The fucking *one*.

I'm a believer.

If I thought I was in love with her before, it's nothing compared to what I feel now. After what we just spent the last three hours doing. After seeing what's on her back, every line an arrow directing my heart toward its home.

I've been with a lot of women. I've even loved some of them. But this is different. So fucking different. What we shared was more than sex. Every part of me came apart inside her, in her skin, her mouth, her gasps and sighs. And then she put me back together with slow, lingering kisses, trailing fingertips, and soft smiles.

Unable to help myself, I drag a fingertip lightly over the lowest lines of her tattoo—waves and rocks nestled in the curve just above the delicious swell of her ass.

Sophie stirs, stretching a little. "I guess the cat's out of the bag." Her voice is raspy and a total turn-on since I know it's partly from making her scream. Multiple times.

She turns toward me, blinking sleepily, candlelight caressing her beautiful face. "Is it weird? That they're so similar? I already had the outline done when I saw your back six years ago."

My lips twitch. "I bet that was a shock."

She nods, mouth curving. "Not an entirely unpleasant one, though."

"It's not weird. Or if it is, it's my kind of weird. I like it. A lot."

Whatever she hears in my voice makes her eyes darken. Shifting back on the bed, she nestles her ass against my rapidly hardening cock.

I wrap an arm around her middle and pull her against my chest, dropping my mouth to her neck. "I can't get enough of you," I whisper between kisses. "You smell so good. You taste so good." I roll my hips forward, sliding my cock between her thighs, and groan. "You're already wet for me."

"Mmm. I'm also sore. Very, very sore." I start to pull away, but she throws a hand back, gripping my hip. "I didn't say stop. Just go slow."

My heart drums against my chest as I thrust into the sheath of her thighs. Every one of my senses is hyper-aware of her—the scent of her arousal, the way her breathing deepens before going choppy. I stroke the curve of her waist and hip, then tease her breasts, cued to every hitch of breath that tells me what she likes.

"Inside me," she pants, "now."

"Yes, ma'am," I murmur, nibbling her neck as I carefully sink into her wet, tight heat. "Oh, fuck. I swear you feel better every time."

"Agreed," she breathes.

I fill her slowly, moving as carefully as I'm capable of, pausing every few seconds so she can adjust. I feel like a teenager, my balls already tight and ready to explode.

"I think your pussy was custom-made for me," I mumble.

She giggles, which does interesting things to my cock. I blow out a slow breath, wondering how the hell I got this lucky in life.

"Are you going to move, or just hang out in there?"

I bite her neck playfully, then drag my nose over her ear. "If you want it, take it."

In five seconds flat, I'm on my back and she's lowering herself onto me, a goddess with messy hair and a body made for me. Her palms plant on my chest as she lifts up and slowly impales herself again. The look on her face is enthralling—a mix of fascination, lust, and sheer delight. She grinds against me, and the cutest expression of wonderment captures her features.

"Matt," she whispers, her eyes wide on mine, voice a little high. There's a question in my name—one I've already answered for myself.

But she's not ready to hear it.

My hand sliding to the back of her neck, I draw her

toward me. "It's okay," I tell her between kisses. "I'm right here. Feeling the same things you're feeling."

I roll my hips slowly upward. She whimpers, trembling, so I do it again, and again, until she comes with a strangled cry into my mouth. The pulsing squeezes on my cock are all it takes for me to let go, too.

Sophie collapses onto my chest, her heartbeat bumping against mine. Her fingers toy with the hair behind my ear. Mine stroke along her spine and sides.

"Don't say it, Matt. Don't even think it."

Her whisper is almost too soft for me to hear. But I do. And I know exactly what she means because I feel it in my chest like a giant's hand is fisted around my heart.

I kiss the top of her head. "I won't."

It's the first—and hopefully last—lie I'll ever tell her.

22

"*H*ey, Mom, do you have a minute?" She reacts immediately to my question, dropping the book she's reading to her lap and fixing her hazel eyes on my face. Her carefully neutral expression belies the fear in her eyes, which punches me with guilt.

"It's nothing major," I say quickly.

Her eyes swiftly clear. Smiling warmly, she pats the cushion next to her. "Sit with me."

I cross the living room and sit next to her on the saggy couch we've had for two decades. Her arm wraps around my shoulders. I lean into her, inhaling her familiar floral fragrance.

The house, for once, is quiet, with only soft music coming from Beka's room upstairs. Our Saturday morning breakfast wrapped up thirty minutes ago, and I just finished cleaning the kitchen. Josh split for a tattoo appointment after eating, and Patrick left right after him to do God knows what with his new girlfriend.

"Have you met Patrick's newest?" I ask.

"Not yet, but he's smitten."

I snort. "He's smitten once a month. What he needs is to fall in love with a better paying job. Part-time front desk at a gym isn't cutting it."

She hums her agreement. "Let me guess—he asked you for money?"

"Yeah. He did the puppy face and everything. I gave him what was in my wallet." At her soft chuckle, I sigh. "He hit you up, too."

"Oh, yes. Swindled me out of forty bucks. Pretty sure he buttered up Josh, as well."

I exhale a silent laugh. "That little crook."

"He's a hopeless romantic, our Patrick," she says wistfully. "What he actually needs is to find a girlfriend who likes him for who he is, not because he buys her things."

In the silence that follows, neither of us addresses the elephant in the room: how much money, and lack thereof, has shaped our lives—choices, patterns, personalities—the last sixteen years.

My mom clears her throat. "What did you want to talk about, sweetheart?"

Knowing it's too late to back out without making her worry, I sit up and face her. "I actually have a weird question. You don't have to answer if you don't want to."

Her brows lift. "Okay. Now I'm curious."

I blow out a breath, fiddling with a small hole on the thigh of my jeans. "It's about you and Dad."

Emotion ripples across her features before it's smoothed away with a smile. "Let's hear it. You know I love talking about George."

"But it hurts you, too," I whisper, grabbing her hand. "I'm sorry."

She grips my fingers tightly. "Of course it hurts, Sophie, but talking about him is a good pain. More sweetness than sorrow. I never want you to feel like you can't talk to me about him."

I nod a few times, trying to keep my shit together while a part of me wants to sob for a man I don't even remember. "I was thinking about him—about you both —last night, and, uh, I was wondering... you guys were so young when you got married and had kids. How did you know? That he was your person? Were you always happy? If he hadn't died, do you think you'd still be together?" I finally look up into my mom's surprised eyes.

"Oh, wow." She sits up, smoothing flyaway hairs in her ponytail, then faces me with a soft smile. "Those are some big questions. Let's see. How did I know he was my person? The oversimplified answer is that I loved him. He wasn't perfect, your father—and Lord knows neither was I—but we loved each other in spite of our flaws."

"But what did it feel like?"

Her perceptive gaze narrows on me, but thankfully she doesn't ask me *why* I'm asking. At length, she says, "This is going to sound odd, but I don't think I knew what love was—what I truly had with your dad—until after your stepfather left us. Granted, I've had a lot of time in the last decade to reflect." She shrugs. "Maybe it's not something you *can* know when you're young and deep in the chaos of day-to-day life."

I frown, not following, but she just squeezes my hand. "You asked me what it felt like. In retrospect, it felt like safety. Not external but emotional. Were George and I always happy? No, of course not. But our ups and downs were with life, not with each other. Understand?"

"I think so."

She smiles slightly. "When you love someone, you want to spend your bad days with them just as much as your good. They're the person you seek out in pain as much as in happiness. Something deep inside you sighs with relief, finally relaxing only when their arms are around you. Would your dad and I still be together today? I like to think so, but ultimately, I can't answer that question. But I can tell you I miss him every day, that there's still no one else I'd rather grow old with."

"And you didn't feel that way with Rodger?" I whisper his name with a glance at the stairs.

She laughs lightly, but the skin around her eyes tightens. "We're really getting deep, aren't we?"

"You don't have to—"

"No, it's okay." She stares out the window at the small front yard. "I thought I did. At first. But by the time Beka was born, I had pretty much resigned myself to never feeling that way again."

"I'm sorry, Mom."

Her eyes return to me. "It's all right, sweetheart. I'm glad we're at the point where we can have these conversations." She hesitates. "I have to ask—does this mean there's someone in your life?"

My gaze drops again. "I think... *Shit.* Maybe. Yes. I think I have feelings for someone. And I think he has feelings for me. But I don't know how to trust any of it."

"Of course you don't," she says, her eyes flooding with tears. "Your dad died, your stepfather split, and someone you thought loved you betrayed you in the most vile way. If you didn't have issues with men, I'd think you were a robot." She stifles a sob. "One of my biggest regrets is not getting you and Josh into therapy when you were teenagers. I wonder a lot if it would have prevented—"

"Mom, no," I interrupt, grabbing her and pulling her into my arms. "That was *not* your fault. Not even remotely."

I know what happened to me haunts her. I know she feels like it's her fault, like she should have seen the signs. It's the curse of motherhood—the impossible expectation that you should be able to prevent your child from suffering in life. There's nothing I can do to change it except tell her, over and over, that I survived.

"I'm here," I whisper. "I'm safe. I'm okay. Promise."

"I know," she whispers, "I know, darling. I'm so grateful, so glad. You're such an incredible woman. The strongest person I know."

I kiss her soft cheek. "Ditto."

23

Four days. Just four days have passed since Matt and I threw a grenade on our *just friends* policy. Four days of feeling like I've slipped into another timeline, one where I come home at night to a man in my apartment. Sitting on the couch with Pickle. Cooking barefoot in my tiny kitchen. Watching television. Reading a book in my bed. Browsing through my sketchbooks—thankfully, I had the foresight to hide the ones filled with him.

When I get home from work Saturday night, however, my apartment is empty. Even though Matt forewarned me he wouldn't be here, it still hits like a sucker punch—how fast I got used to sharing space with him. How natural it felt coming home and finding him here.

Even Pickle's meowed greeting seems sad, his tail-twitching not as sassy as usual. I pick him up and cross to the couch, where he lets me pet him for approximately six seconds before jumping off my lap and strutting back to the front door. He sits, his back to me, eyes on the door.

"Pathetic," I tell him.

Pulling my phone from my pocket, I take a quick photo of Pickle's shame and send it to Matt. Then I turn on the TV. Turn it back off. Put away the dishes on the drying rack. Make a cup of tea. Light a few candles. Consider drawing. Discard the idea. Open a book. Close it after a minute when I can't comprehend a single sentence.

I call Kelly, desperate for a distraction, but when she doesn't answer, I remember it's Saturday night. She's either at a bar or doing something else fun, because unlike me, she has a thriving social life.

My unease grows side by side with uncomfortable, unfamiliar feelings and thoughts.

Is he thinking about me?

Does he miss me?

My phone starts vibrating with an incoming call. I lunge for it and grin when I see his name. I'm thrilled. Euphoric. And in the next second, my own reaction dismays and terrifies me.

I'm an absolute mess.

Don't be an idiot. Just answer.

"Hi." I miss the mark on calm by a few miles, my voice high and strangled-sounding.

"Hi back. How was work? Are you wearing clothes?"

I laugh in spite of myself. "Work was fine. Just got home a few minutes ago, so yes, I'm still clothed."

"Bummer. I miss you."

My heart hiccups. "I, um, miss you too."

He laughs softly. "Not as much as Pickle does, apparently."

Desperate to talk about anything other than feelings, I ask quickly, "How was the surprise party?"

"Perfect. Mom was totally shocked." He chuckles. "Erin and I didn't think Bill would be able to keep the secret, but he did. You should have seen her face. It was classic. She was so surprised I think she forgot how many times she told us she didn't want to celebrate turning sixty. I'm sure she'll remember and chew us out tomorrow."

I laugh. There's a beep and a rustle as the Bluetooth car audio switches to his phone. A door opens and closes.

"Still there, Dollface?"

"Yep, are you home?"

"Almost. I have a bunch of stuff in my hands, though, so can you open the front door?"

My heart free falls. I jump off the couch just as Pickle starts meowing and pull open the door so fast I almost launch the poor cat across the room. He yowls in affront as I poke my head into the hallway to see Matt walking toward me.

"Hi," he says, eyes twinkling as he reaches my door. "I probably should have asked if I could come over."

"But you didn't," I whisper.

He bites his lip and shakes his head, then lifts a reusable tote. "Want some leftover baked ziti and chocolate cake?"

I grab a fistful of his sweatshirt and pull him into the apartment, kicking the door closed with my foot. The bag hits the floor and then his mouth is on mine, his hands cupping my ass as he lifts me off the floor and shuffle-walks backward to the couch. When he hits the arm, he falls backward with me atop him.

I whip his sweatshirt and shirt off, then attack his jeans as he pulls up my skirt and fumbles under the waistband of my tights. Our seeking fingers find what they want at the same time, and we moan in unison.

"Take these stupid things off," he mumbles against my neck as he tugs at my tights.

Laughing soundlessly, I stand up only long enough

to pull off my tights and sweater, then straddle him again just as he gets his jeans and boxers over his hips. Wasting no time, I sink slowly down, sheathing him inside my body one thick inch at a time.

"Fuck," he growls into my mouth, hips jerking up and stealing my breath. "I thought about this all day. If there was a way to live inside this pussy twenty-four seven, I would."

I laugh, which makes him groan. His arms come around my back, gripping my hips to hold me still as he fucks me from below. My eyes roll back in my head, all thoughts vanishing beneath the sensory tidal wave.

"Look at me, Sophie."

Opening my eyes takes effort, and I almost close them again when I see his perfect face, those blue eyes fixed on me with burning intensity. Instead, I capture his lips, sucking his tongue into my mouth. He tastes like chocolate and smells like a windswept coast, so perfect it's suddenly too much—my orgasm hits like a bolt of lightning, racing from my fingers and toes to my center in a second flat. I cry out as my body clamps down. His thrusts grow erratic before he stiffens, his cock pulsing as he empties himself inside me. I shiver at the sensation, aftershocks rippling through me.

My face tucked into his neck, I relearn how to breathe, slowly becoming aware that I'm still wearing my skirt and bra, and his pants are tangled around his knees.

"Holy shit," he gasps, squeezing me gently, his lips against my hair. "That was intense. I love—d it." The trip in his words is minor, the recovery seamless, but it feels like a bucket of cold water.

My breath stalls.

He stiffens minutely. "Sophie—"

"I loved it, too," I say quickly, then give him a kiss before slowly lifting myself off him and pulling my skirt down. My legs feel wobbly as I make my way to the bathroom and close the door.

"Don't overthink it," I tell myself. "It doesn't mean what you think it means. What it could mean. Everything is fine."

I stare at my flushed face in the mirror, taking in my dazed, slightly crazed eyes and tousled hair.

A memory of his voice whispers through my head: *"I'm already half in love with you, Sophie."*

I splash freezing water on my face until I'm grounded back in the present, then head to my bedroom to shuck off the rest of my clothes and pull on pajamas. When I return to the living room, Matt's in the kitchen, jeans pulled up but unbuttoned. He glances up from plating two slices of chocolate cake, which don't look nearly as delicious as he does shirtless with his hair askew from my hands.

He grins. "How are you so cute?"

I glance down at my flannel pajamas, flushing as I realize I hadn't been thinking when I pulled on my oldest, coziest set out of the drawer.

"Uhh..."

"You're literally the sexist thing I've ever seen, and I'm the luckiest man on Earth."

My face grows even hotter. "Ew. Stop."

He laughs, deep and infectious, and brings the plates to the coffee table. "Come eat some cake. I promise I won't compliment you again for at least ten minutes."

I comply, moaning around the first bite of decadent chocolate. "This is so good." I lick the fork before spearing another piece, then glance at Matt.

His heavy-lidded gaze lifts from my lips. Knowing exactly what he's thinking, I squirm at the painful ache between my thighs.

"I'll happily give you a blowjob," I tell him, "but my vagina is on strike. No giant dicks allowed."

He chokes on a swallow of cake, then laughs heartily and grabs my face for a messy, chocolatey kiss.

24

---

*I*t's late. After 2:00 a.m. My head rests on his chest, my arm listless over his waist, my leg nestled between both of his. His hand strokes the hair down my back in gentle, ceaseless caresses.

If I were a cat, I'd be purring.

"Next summer." His quiet voice vibrates in the dark. "Do you have plans?"

It takes my fuzzy brain a few moments to process. Lifting my head, I peer at his shadowed face, noting he doesn't look nearly as sleepy as I am.

"Summer plans? Matt, I don't even have plans for next week."

His lips curve as he glances down at me. "Me neither. Only asking because we finalized next year's schedule. South by Southwest in March and Boston Calling in May."

"Oh, no big deal," I say dryly. "Just two of the biggest music festivals in the country."

"I'm a big deal, Dollface."

I laugh and lightly pinch his waist. He chuckles and kisses my head.

"After May, though, we're tour-free for at least seven months. Rose is due in mid July, and Julian was adamant about taking the time off. We all agreed, obviously. I know Julian will keep writing songs—I don't think he knows how to stop—but we won't do any more recording until the following year. The album we're working on now is going on pause, too, because he wants to focus on Rose."

Something in his voice makes me sit up a little, leaning on my elbow so I can see his face. "How are you feeling about that?"

His eyes meet mine. "Excited. Relieved." He pauses. "Fucking scared. We've taken breaks before, but this one feels different." He laughs a little. "Julian is going to be a dad."

"Yeah, that's a pretty huge life event." I hesitate. "Are you worried he's not going to want to come back to the band?"

He shakes his head. "Nah. Breaking Giants is in his blood. In all of our blood. We're lifers."

I rub my cheek against his chest, placing a kiss on the warm skin. "What's scaring you?"

He stares at the ceiling, brow furrowed. "Nothing definitive. Maybe just the general sense of things changing, new phases of life beginning, you know?" Stirring, he rolls to face me, a hot palm resting against my cheek. "Enough of my existential bullshit. I asked about next summer because I want to take you somewhere for a couple weeks. Bali, Sweden, France... wherever you want to go. First class all the way. Just you and me."

My lungs squeeze with sudden pressure; discomfort prickles in my limbs. I know, *know*, it's an unhealthy reaction to the incredibly romantic and generous offer, but I have zero control over my body's response. Suddenly claustrophobic, I scoot back and sit up, then lean over when a wave of dizziness hits me.

"Hey, are you okay?" The concern in his voice grates.

"Yeah," I force out. "Just... need some water."

I jump off the bed and make it into the bathroom, closing and locking the door behind me. Then I sink down to the tile and focus on breathing past the pressure in my chest. My vision tunnels, bright spots sparkling along the edges. My heart pounds a merciless cadence inside my throat. Cold sweat breaks out on my forehead, my neck, my back.

I haven't had a panic attack this bad in years.

"Fuck, fuck," I whisper, pressing the heels of my hands into my eyes. I start counting my breaths, forcing my lungs to expand for four seconds. Hold four seconds. Exhale four seconds.

I'm on the third round when the wood against my spine jolts slightly as Matt sits on the other side. A second later, Pickle meeps and his fuzzy paw darts under the door, a game I call Whack a Paw that normally makes me laugh.

This time, it's not enough to quell my panic. Not with the source so close. My breath falters, my efforts at box breathing falling short.

"Tell me what to do," Matt says, his voice raw with worry and pain.

"I-I can't," I whisper back. "It's not your fault. This is... it's too much."

"Okay. I promise to never take you on vacation." The forced levity in his voice brings tears to my eyes. He's trying. God, he's trying so hard to be what I need.

But I'm caught in a dark undertow, my thoughts spiraling. I keep envisioning his face as he talked about next year, about Julian becoming a dad—I keep hearing the longing beneath the words. His avoidance when I asked him what was scaring him.

Because I know.

Deep down, I know.

Until four months ago, he was getting married in March. He wanted—*still wants*—to be married. He wants to embrace the next phase of his life. Start a family. Be a father. Live happily ever after in his giant house. Go on exotic vacations.

First class all the way.

Beads of sweat roll down my neck, my back, my temple. I shudder, curling forward until my knees squeeze against my temples. Hard. Harder. I gasp for breath, a fish out of water.

A woman out of her mind.

A small part of me knows my darkness might be feeding me false narratives to protect my heart, but there's another possibility—it's merely filling in the blanks about why he latched on to me so fast. Why he thinks he's in love with me.

He's obeying a deep need to replace what he lost.

A wife.

"Sophie," he whispers thickly. "Please talk to me."

"I can't—I'm not—I'm not *her*, Matt." A dam inside me breaks, my voice steadying. "I'm not wife and mother material. If that's what you want, what you need, then you have to go. We have to stop."

He's silent for a long time. Too long. Sorrow is an anchor that sinks my heart to the floor. Strangely, it also drags my panic attack away with it, clearing my head and deepening my breath—breath that's now thick with tears.

"I won't lie and say I haven't thought about a future with you," he says finally. "But believe it or not, I've never felt this way about anyone before, and definitely never this fast. It's... overwhelming. I want to be around you all the time. I think about you constantly. I feel better around you, like I can be myself. I never have to put on an act."

He pauses. There's a thud as his head hits the door. "I've fucked up. The last four days have been too intense. I'm smothering you. And the timing of everything... I can understand why you might think I'm rebounding from Melody, but all I can do is promise you I'm not. This—everything about you, us—is different." The door moves again as he stands. "I don't want to leave, but I think you need me to. You have to come out, though. I need to see your face and know you're okay."

Swiping tears from my cheeks, I stand on unsteady feet and open the door. Tortured blue eyes roam my features, searching for reassurance.

"I'm fine." My voice is too sharp, but I can't help it. I hate the fear in his eyes. I hate that it's because he knows about my scars, because he's scared for my safety.

I want to scream.

Instead, a caustic laugh burns my throat. "Do you realize how fucked-up this is?" I gesture at my body, soaked with panic sweat. "How could you possibly want to deal with this, Matt?"

He swallows hard, his jaw tensing. "You made me promise not to say it."

I squeeze my eyes shut, clenching my teeth and pressing my tongue to the roof of my mouth like I can force his admission back out of my ears.

"What happened eight years ago happened to a different person. You don't have to worry about me." I open my eyes. "Just go. I'll be fine."

"Are you ending this, Sophie?" he asks, his eyes guarded, voice almost monotone.

My heart goes toe-to-toe with my darkness. A vicious battle begins and ends in the space of a breath, my heart winning by the slightest margin.

"No," I say, and his face relaxes. "I just need a little space."

The slightest smile curves his lips, but shadows still lurk in his eyes. "I can work with that. Get some sleep, okay? Give me a call when... whenever you want to."

I nod and watch him disappear into the bedroom, then close the bathroom door and lean my forehead on it. A minute later, his steps come back down the hallway, pausing only long enough for him to say, "Lock it behind me."

"I will," I whisper.

The front door opens. Closes.

Pickle gives a sad, warbly meow.

lki Beach is dreary, the weather freezing cold and wet. Midmorning clouds hang dense and low, emitting moisture too thick to be mist and too misty to be classified as rain.

My lungs are on fire, my muscles screaming. Not because of the cold, but because my psychotic brother has set a brutal pace for our run. I used to join him more regularly—especially when we lived together—but in the last few years, I've grown overly fond of sleeping late and lazing about before my afternoon shifts.

The only reason I'm subjecting myself willingly to this torture is because I woke up this morning and couldn't stand being in my apartment, the walls bursting with reminders of *him*.

"You're seriously out of shape, Soph," says Josh, his

voice almost normal despite the fact we're working on mile four at the moment.

"Fuck off," I gasp.

He laughs. "Correct me if I'm wrong, but wasn't it *you* who showed up at *my* door and asked to go for a run?"

"Stop. Talking. I'll. Puke."

He shuts his mouth. An indeterminable amount of time later—AKA an eternity—he slows to a walk and finally stops. As he stretches, I heave for air with my hands on my knees. Eventually, the blood stops pounding behind my eyeballs and the urge to lose my breakfast fades. I straighten, wiping the sheet of mingled sweat and rain off my face. While Josh continues being annoying as hell with his fancy stretches, I plop my wet butt onto an equally wet log.

When he's done stretching his quads, he sits beside me. "Okay, tell me what's wrong."

I stare at the gray water. Gray, gray, everything is gray. "Nothing. I just wanted to exercise."

"Bullshit. You're squirrelly. Do I need to beat the shit out of Matt?"

My gaze jerks to his face. He's serious. "No," I say quickly.

"Thank God. He'd wipe the floor with me."

I laugh in spite of myself. "No beatings necessary on my account. He's been really good to me."

So good I freaked the fuck out.

"Does that mean you're actually dating?" he asks flatly.

I shrug and twitch in place, uncomfortable for reasons that have nothing to do with my soaking wet running clothes. "We're... more than friends. I don't know if it has a label at this point."

Josh heaves a sigh. "What's going on in your head, Soph? I know you didn't come running for fun."

Rain mists from my mouth as I blow out a breath. I mumble, "I think he's serious about me. Being with me."

"Okay," he says slowly. "That makes me want to kill him less. Why is this bad?"

"Because, Joshy... I'm *me*. Last night, he invited me to go on a fancy vacation with him next summer and I had a full-blown panic attack. Sweating, hyperventilating, the whole thing. He probably wants me to meet his family. He said he thinks about our future. I think he almost told me he loves me."

Josh blinks at me a few times, his expression blank before a slow smile overtakes his wet face. "Holy shit," he murmurs, head shaking. "I'm an idiot."

"What are you babbling about?"

"You two." He laughs shortly. "It makes sense. You're actually fucking perfect for each other."

I stand up so fast my legs almost collapse in retribution. "We're not, though! Don't you get it? I'm a fucking train wreck! He's ready for the real shit—weddings and babies and fucking vacations! He doesn't want me, he wants a cookie-cutter wife! And here I am, Stranger Danger Central with CPTSD!"

My brother stares calmly at me. "Are you done screaming at me?"

I sag back onto the log. "Yes."

"First off—are we talking about the same Matt Sullivan? The freak of genetics who could basically land any woman he wants?"

I gape. "What the fuck, Josh! How does that help?"

He rolls his eyes. "If what you're saying is true—and I'm not saying it is—but if you're as big of a mess as you think you are, then why would he be talking about six months from now with you? Why would he waste his time?"

I open my mouth, but he cuts me off.

"Matt's not an idiot. You've been hanging out for months. If he didn't want to be with you, he wouldn't be. Unless you've been putting on some elaborate mask this whole time, acting like someone you're not?"

"No," I whisper. "He knows the truth about what

happened. And after last night, he's pretty much seen everything."

He bumps my shoulder with his. "You've been safe for a long time, Sophie. You've built yourself a nice little prison to keep yourself that way."

"Suck a dick, Josh," I mutter without heat. We've had this conversation before—him communicating his concern that I've allowed fear to make my world small. Safe, but confining and colorless.

"Keeping with my brilliant prison metaphor," he adds with enough glee to make me scowl. "It seems to me that since meeting Matt, you've been tunneling your way out without even realizing it."

I stare at him. Then I stare at the water. The sky. The sand clinging to my damp sneakers. Finally, I say, "I'm never running with you again. This sucks."

He laughs and hauls me to my feet. "Come on, let's get dry. I'll buy you lunch."

"Damn right you will."

BY THE END of my shift, I'm wrung out physically and mentally. Despite a shower before work and periodic ibuprofen consumption, I'm sore as hell.

On the emotional front, conversely, I feel surprisingly calm thanks to Josh's patented method of simultaneously comforting me and calling me out. What he said made sense, and I cling to the logic like it's a life raft.

I'm still scared. So scared of what's happening between Matt and me. What it means. What the future holds.

But perhaps Josh's lame prison metaphor isn't far from the truth. Without really being aware of it, since meeting Matt, I've been tunneling out of my dark cell.

Unfortunately, for someone trapped in a cage for years, fresh air and the sky is more terrifying than the familiar darkness.

I need to call him. I know I do. But when I get home, I hesitate. Procrastinate. I take another shower, then curl up on the couch and check my account balances. I pay a few bills, tweak my budgeting app, and do my best not to think about hiking in Switzerland with Matt. How it's been a dream of mine to go there. How I'd resigned myself to never being able to afford it.

Eventually, my fear of contacting him is outweighed by the simple fact *I miss him*. For better or worse, he wormed his way into my life so completely that he's exactly what he said he'd be: my best friend.

He answers on the second ring. "Hi."

The deep, intimate timbre of his voice melts my

insides. I wait a beat for my lungs to reform from puddles of goo.

"Hey." My voice is weak. "How are you?"

"I'm okay," he says softly. "How are you?"

"Okay. Good." I pause. "I went for a run with Josh this morning, which was a mistake."

"Oh, shit." He chuckles. "I made the same mistake once. He dragged me ten miles. Your brother is an animal. Can you walk?"

I smile. "So far, yes. Tomorrow will be worse for sure."

"You should sit in my hot tub for an hour. It would help." He hesitates. "Next time, or whenever."

"Thanks," I say quickly. "I'll definitely do that. Maybe, uh, tomorrow? After I get off work?"

I hear his breath sigh through the line. "Sounds good. I'll be here. Want dinner, too?"

"Yes, please."

"You got it."

I can't contain my smile. "Okay. It's a date."

There's another lengthy pause. "A date?" he asks carefully.

My heart patters faster. "Yes. I, uh... I'm wondering if you want to start, you know, *dating*. Not as friends. Or friends who have sex."

"Sophie." My name rides a breath laden with intensity. "Are you asking me to be your boyfriend?"

I swallow hard. "Yes. I am. And if we're still together next summer, I'd really like to go to Switzerland."

"Oh, we'll be together," he answers in a low voice. "The answer is yes. One thousand percent, yes. I'd love to be your boyfriend."

The pulse in my chest navigates south, and I bite my lips on the impulse to tell him to come over *right fucking now*.

"Great. Cool. Sounds good."

His warm laughter coats my ear.

26

The following weeks bleed together in a haze of happiness. Some things stay the same—work, Saturday at Mom's, meetups with Kelly—but the rest of my time is spent with Matt.

We have long, lingering dates at restaurants around town with incredible food and intimate settings. We check out up-and-coming bands he's heard a rumor about. One Friday, there's a double date with Nick and Kat, and the next Thursday we bring tamales to an impromptu potluck at Julian and Rose's house. They welcome me into their lives; especially Rose, who takes me under her quirky, pregnancy-addled wing.

Most nights are spent at my apartment—Matt won't admit it, but I think it's because he worries that Pickle is lonely when we aren't there. I don't complain, though. I like having him in my space. So much that I give him a drawer in my dresser and a shelf in my bathroom cabinet, both decisions ones I refuse to dwell on.

Once in a while—usually after sex that inexplicably keeps getting better and better—I feel myself shutting down emotionally. Old fears ignite. Doubts creep in. And in those moments, Matt will give me a kiss on the forehead and quietly slip away, usually to the living room to watch a show or read.

I do my box breathing. Sometimes I sketch or take a shower or bath. I don't have any more full-blown panic attacks. And when the feelings pass, I find him and curl up beside him. He strokes my hair and kisses my forehead. Makes me tea and asks what show or movie I want to watch.

He doesn't push me to talk about it, or about the future, or the fact we went from agreeing to date to practically living together. We exist in a delicate bubble that neither of us wants to pop.

And the days go on.

My weekend off is right before Thanksgiving and is spent in a time warp back to a childhood I never had: Saturday night Matt takes me roller skating again, and we spend Sunday at a year-round amusement park playing arcade games, bumper cars, and laser tag. We eat cotton candy and too much ice cream, take cheesy photo-booth photos and give our game prizes to gawking kids. We hold hands and make out like teenagers, and laugh until our stomachs hurt.

I work Monday through Wednesday. The night before Thanksgiving, we stay up late making four pies. Two for my mom. Two for his. At 1:00 p.m. on Thursday, as we walk up the path to his parents' front door, laughter is the furthest thing from my mind.

I feel like I'm going to puke.

I don't really remember *how* or *when* I agreed to the dual insanity of meeting each other's families for the first time on a giant holiday, but here we are. He probably asked me after giving me multiple orgasms—he's smart like that.

"Trust me, they'll love you."

I pull at the neck of my sweater, wishing I'd opted for something other than wool. It's frigid outside, but my anxiety is a furnace beneath my skin.

As much as his words reassure, I can tell he's nervous, too. Rose's words from months ago float back to me, *"Melody didn't get along with his family."*

Before I can do something stupid like chuck my pie on the grass and run back to the car, the front door opens. My first glimpse of Matt's mom tells me where he got his looks. She's close to six feet tall, statuesque and undeniably gorgeous, with bright blue eyes and a giant smile I recognize. Shockingly, she also looks on the outside how I feel on the inside.

Like a certified hot mess.

Her pale blond hair is in a haphazard bun that lists to one side. Over jeans and a lavender sweater with a hole in one arm, she wears a faded yellow apron that's mottled with bleach stains and streaks of pink I'm hoping are cranberry sauce.

Ignoring her son, she rushes toward me. Matt grabs my pie a second before his mom's arms wrap around me and squeeze. She smells like cranberries and sugar, and my face smooshes against her chest like I'm a child.

Weirdly, I don't freak out. Even more amazingly, all my anxiety melts away and I hug her back, trying not to laugh.

Arms still looped around me, she leans back enough to see my face, blue eyes bright and roaming. "Sophie, Sophie, it's so wonderful to meet you." Her voice retains a slight accent, and I recall Matt telling me she moved to the States from Sweden with her family when she was a teen. "You're even more beautiful than Matt said you were."

A dull heat crawls up my neck. "It's great to meet you, too, Mrs. Sullivan."

She winks. "Call me Vera. Please."

Matt's laugh is a bit strained. "Let her go, Mom."

Laughing, Vera releases me. Matt opens his arms quickly, a pie balanced on each hand as she wraps him in a tight embrace. "My sweet baby," I hear her murmur. "I'm so proud of you."

"Erin!" booms a voice from the house. "Matt and Sophie are here!"

Seconds later, we're joined by a tall, rail-thin man with a head full of silver hair and thick glasses, and a smiling younger woman I place easily as his sister, Erin. They introduce themselves, both of them huggers, then usher me into the house with my arms in theirs, chattering nonstop.

I glance back at Matt to see him watching me with an alarmed expression, and quickly mouth, "I'm fine."

A smile blooms on his face, his eyes caressing my features with a tender look I've come to crave.

Beside him, Vera watches, smiling like she has a secret. And as much as I've refused to acknowledge it over the last few weeks, I know exactly what the secret is.

"I LOVE YOUR FAMILY," I tell Matt, yawning in the darkness of our drive home. The hum of the road is lulling me toward sleep as surely as the back-to-back Thanksgiving dinners.

His fingers, entwined in mine atop his thigh, tighten. "They're nuts," he says with a chuckle.

"A little, but so is mine."

I roll my head to the side to see his profile and watch as his lips curve. "Your mom is amazing. Beka is great, so smart and sweet. And Patrick is a trip—he kind of reminds me of me at that age."

"You were terminally full of yourself, too?"

He laughs. "A bit. But more like he has all this energy and doesn't quite know what to do with it. Has he ever picked up an instrument?"

"Pretty much all of them. He loves music—especially punk and post-punk from the seventies and eighties. He's also one of those annoying people who can learn any instrument in a few weeks. But he's easily bored and never sticks to anything."

"Maybe he needs to find a band."

I smile. "Josh and I have told him that a thousand times, but I have a feeling if I tell him *you* suggested it, he might actually do it. In case you missed it, he ignored his girlfriend the whole time to follow you around like a puppy and hang on your every word."

He winces in embarrassment. "I did notice. I also

noticed that Josh didn't try to take me outside and rough me up, which was a pleasant surprise."

I hum in agreement. "He knows how happy you make me." *Now my whole family knows,* I add privately. I definitely didn't miss the knowing, giddy looks my mom and Beka kept throwing my way all evening.

Matt parks outside my apartment and turns in his seat. "Do I?" he asks quietly, eyes on mine. "Make you happy?"

"Yes, Matthew," I whisper.

We make it into the apartment before we embarrass ourselves in public. Within a minute, our clothes are in a pile and my back hits the hallway wall. My legs tight around his hips, he slides inside me slowly, so slowly my body feels wound impossibly tight, humming at a feverish pitch.

I make a small noise. He knows what I need, thrusting hard and deep, grinding his pelvis against mine.

I see stars.

"Sophie," he whispers tightly against my neck.

"Don't say it," I gasp.

He growls in frustration and strides swiftly into my bedroom, dropping us onto the bed without breaking the contact of our bodies. Then he takes out his angst on my willing body, with possessive, domineering hands and brutally deep thrusts.

I end up on all fours, his chest to my back. One of his hands is braced on the bed beside mine. The other rests low on my abdomen, fingers circling expertly on my clit while his palm applies pressure that pushes his cock against the most sensitive place inside me.

He's everywhere. Around, throughout, above, below, permeating every part of me.

I'm utterly lost. Consumed.

"Let me have it," he rasps against my ear. "All of it. Come for me, baby."

I do, muffling my scream against a pillow as my orgasm unfolds like a seafloor cataclysm that swallows us both.

27

The day my darkness returns—the second Friday in December—begins normally enough with a cup of coffee on my couch and a phone call from Matt, who left yesterday for a four-day trip to Palm Springs with Nick and Jackson.

The three of them make the trip every year before Christmas sans Julian, who said at dinner last week that he'd rather cut off his own balls than "be around a bunch of desperate drunks gambling." Matt just laughed and said nowadays they don't even gamble that much, and instead spend most of their time lounging in the sun, embarrassing themselves on golf courses and getting massages and fancy spa treatments.

"Do you miss me?" he asks, his sleepy voice making me smile.

"You know I do," I tell him. "You guys stay out late last night?"

He yawns loudly. "We actually came back to the house after dinner, but ended up drinking and playing cards until four. I took all their money."

I laugh. "Good for you. Now go back to sleep."

"Mmm, think I will. It's weird sleeping without cuddling you, though. You're my human stuffed animal."

I laugh. "Wow."

"Call me when you get off?" he asks with a smile in his voice.

"Won't you be out?"

"Why would that matter? Call me, Dollface."

"Okay, Matthew."

We hang up, and my phone reconnects to my Bluetooth speaker, filling my apartment with the soft, atmospheric music I listen to while drawing. The world outside is a dull blur behind sheets of rain. Pickle rests against my thigh, a warm lump.

I finish my coffee as I work on shading for my current project, a portrait of Beka I want to give her for Christmas. She's a fantasy fanatic and obsessed with elves, so I've elongated her ears and given her a majestic, ethereal crown.

She's gonna flip.

Around noon, I make lunch, then take a quick shower. Get dressed. Say goodbye to Pickle. Turn off the lights and head to work.

A normal day that I don't know yet isn't normal at all.

THE DARKNESS DOESN'T GIVE warnings. It doesn't whisper or knock. It doesn't need to. Smooth as silk, as insubstantial as fog, it lives beneath my skin. In my arteries. My marrow.

I've grown complacent. In the last few months, I've forgotten that it's always with me. A part of me. Patient and waiting. Ready to spill through me like oil, tainting everything it touches.

It happens at exactly 6:54 p.m.

I know the time because I'm in my office on my meal break, scrolling and deleting emails when I read four words.

Google Alert - "Ted Garavito"- - - -

White noise fills my head as it drains of blood. I sway forward, catching myself on the edge of the desk.

My vision blurs, then sharpens, and I press a numb fingertip to the email to open it.

Google Alerts

"Ted Garavito"

NEWS

Five Men Indicted in Tacoma, W.A. in Connection with Sex Trafficking Ring.

I scan the first paragraph of the article, then find what I'm looking for in the second. There are two other names before his, but my brain doesn't register them, only the one I haven't heard in eight years.

…and STEVEN YATES, 37, a/k/a "Ted Garavito," a/k/a "Joe Young," have been charged with Sex Trafficking, multiple counts of Sexual Assault of a Minor, Promoting Prostitution in the Fourth Degree, Conspiracy in the Fourth Degree, and Conspiracy in the Fifth Degree.

My skin pebbles.

My mouth tastes like pennies.

"Steven Yates."

His real name emerges in a choked gasp, his face flashing in my mind. My stomach churns as my lunch from hours ago threatens a reappearance.

I scan the article, zeroing in on one of the last paragraphs.

"These men have a long history of targeting young, vulnerable women and using coercion and ultimately drugs to force them to perform sexual acts with men," said District Attorney Chaplain. "I'm confident that justice will be done, and they'll remain behind bars for the rest of their lives."

"Sophie?"

I lift my head, the movement sluggish, and register Dania standing on the other side of my desk. From her concerned expression, that wasn't the first time she called my name.

"Oh my God, are you all right?"

I shake my head. "No. I, uh... need to go home. Are you and Brian okay to close without me?"

She nods rapidly. "Of course. Should you be driving? Can I call someone?"

Gratitude momentarily lightens the weight on my heart. "Thanks, Dania. Yeah, I'll call my brother."

She heads for the door, pausing on the threshold. "Let me know if you need anything. I'm here for you."

My eyes burn as I nod.

The wave of darkness crests above my head, a thousand feet high, blotting the sky. Dimming my entire world. My survival response is screaming at me to hide, to find a small, defensible burrow to curl up in until danger passes. Every inch of my skin crawls like something vile is about to reach out and touch me. Only the vileness is inside me, and there's no escape.

Dialing Josh takes massive effort, my hand-to-eye coordination almost nonexistent.

"Soph? Aren't you at work?"

A flashback floods my mind. Josh's face, pale and screaming in agony as he hauls me from an overflowing bathtub.

"Sophie?" His voice is sharp now.

"They caught him," I whisper.

"What? Who?" There's a two-second pause in which he figures it out. "They caught that motherfucker? Holy shit. This is great news." Another two-second pause. "Fuck. Okay. You're not okay. Can I pick you up?"

"Yeah."

"I'm on my way." I hear the jangle of car keys. The slam of a door. "Sit tight. I'll be there in ten."

He hangs up. I put my phone in my purse, then hold my bag on my lap, hugging it like a shield.

Time is fluid. My mind is an electrical storm. Floating, numbing clouds interrupted by bright jolts of images. *Memories.* Graphic and revolting. Faces. Hands. Laughter. Pain.

The stains of the past.

The stains in me.

Josh rounds the corner, his hair damp from rain, his

eyes huge as he takes me in. I have no idea what I look like right now, but his green eyes darken with a film of tears that he blinks away.

"Do you want to be touched?" he asks, his gentle voice in marked contrast to the worry in his eyes.

I shake my head.

He straightens and takes a deep breath. I watch as he pulls on a layer of manufactured calm like a coat. "I need you to stand up. Can you do that?"

I nod. It takes me two tries before my legs will hold me.

"You're going to follow right behind me. I'm parked out back. You're safe. I'll be with you." He pauses. "Do you have your pepper spray?"

I nod and dig a hand clumsily through my purse. Gripping the canister, I look back at my brother.

"Good. Follow me. I told the other employees to stay out of the back for a few minutes."

Thank you.

My lips form the words, but no sound comes as the wave breaks over my head and darkness floods into every broken inch of me.

~

MY AWARENESS RETURNS twenty minutes later as Josh hands me a cup of tea. I'm sitting on my couch, Pickle in my lap.

I have no memory past pulling the pepper spray out of my purse.

Shuddering, I lift the tea to my mouth. A tear drips onto my lips, making my first taste of Chamomile salty. There's no associated sadness, though; I'm still a deep water storm. Numb center and spiky corners. Fog and lightning. Wreckage on roiling waters.

I haven't had a psychogenic blackout in close to seven years, thanks to the six months of EMDR therapy Mom and Josh paid for. The treatment didn't free me from the manacle of flashbacks, but over the years, the involuntary recalls of the most horrific time in my life have slowly lost their visceral impact. These days, they're mostly one-dimensional. Sepia and still-frame. Unpleasant but manageable.

Until tonight, that is.

A therapist once told me that the intuitive survival function of the human brain is a violent trauma survivor's greatest ally. Our minds will forever seek to reestablish a healthy baseline, and if we give it the right tools, it will find a new normal.

She also told me that trauma irreversibly changed

my brain, and my 'normal' would never look the same as others'.

I didn't stick with her long, winding up more depressed after our sessions than empowered.

"Are you back with me?" asks Josh softly.

I nod. "Thanks for getting me home."

He sits on the opposite end of the couch and sips his own tea. For a few seconds, I watch his familiar, beloved face, my heart warming with the magnitude of love I feel for him.

"Thank you, Joshy," I whisper, a lifetime of gratitude packed into the three words.

His eyes meet mine, the green swimming in tears that he blinks back. "Don't, please. I'm not in the mood to bawl like a baby." He clears his throat. "I read the article. There's a number at the bottom for the FBI Victim Specialist associated with the case. I'm not saying you should call. Just something to think about at some point."

"Okay. Josh?"

"Mmm?"

"The Chamomile is great, but there's whiskey in the cabinet over the fridge."

He eyes me skeptically, but whatever he sees makes his lips twitch. "All right. As long as we're celebrating—for the most part, at least."

I feel it then, the first weak shaft of sunlight on the surface of the water. Dark clouds press against it, trying to smother it—all the innocent victims, all the suffering he caused others after he was done with me—but the light is still there. Somewhere in the sky, the sun is shining.

They caught him.

My smile is small and vicious. "Oh, we're celebrating."

28

The first thing I hear upon waking is Josh's snoring from the living room couch. The second thing is the persistent vibration of my phone, which by some miracle I remembered to plug in last night.

Groaning, I roll over and grab it off the nightstand, not registering the caller before I answer, "Hello?" My voice is hoarse, my throat raw.

"Sophie?" asks Matt loudly. "Thank fucking God! Are you okay?"

I sit up fast, then clutch my pounding head. My mouth tastes like whiskey and marijuana—the latter courtesy of Josh. "Yeah. Hi." I glance at my clock, then blink. It's five-thirty in the morning. "Why are you calling? Is everything okay?"

"Is everything—" He growls. Actually *growls*. "Are you fucking kidding me right now? You didn't answer my calls all night, then when you finally called me back, you weren't making any fucking sense! I tried reaching Josh, but he wasn't answering. I didn't have your mom's or Kelly's numbers. I almost called the police to do a wellness check!" By the last sentence, he's yelling. He takes a measured breath, voice lowering to tense steel. "I'm at the airport right now, coming home. Just tell me you're okay."

My brain sloshes in my skull even as my stomach sinks like a rock. "I'm okay, Matt," I choke out. "Don't cut your trip short for me."

"It's already done," he snaps, then makes a pained sound. "Do you have any idea how worried I was?"

Tears fill my eyes, burning like acid. "I'm sorry," I say, knowing it's not enough. "I don't remember much from last night. But I was safe. At home. Josh stayed over."

There's a pause in which I hear background noises: announcements from PA systems, muted voices, a baby crying.

Finally, he says, "I'm so mad at you right now." He doesn't sound mad, though. Not anymore. Now he sounds sad, which makes my heart thump fast.

"I'm sorry," I whisper. "I can explain."

"I'll call you when I land."

He hangs up.

I stare at the phone, tears dribbling off my chin, and try to remember what happened last night after I told Josh where the whiskey was. We got drunk. Stupid, fall-on-our-faces drunk. Then we smoked a bowl. Or two or three. I think we watched *Spaceballs* at some point, and I have a vague memory of eating potstickers.

I'd left Josh passed out in the living room and fallen onto my bed. I now remember plugging my phone in and seeing missed calls from Matt; a lot of them. I'd called him back. I recall crying when I heard his voice, and babbling a lot, and...

I gasp. "Oh, fuck me."

I told him I loved him. Over and over, sobbing out the words—and a bunch of others I can't remember—until I abruptly ended the call and passed out.

No wonder he's upset. In fact, he has every right to never want to speak to me again.

It sounded like I was saying goodbye.

I MISS Saturday breakfast for the first time in years. Josh promises to cover for me, dragging himself out of my apartment wearing a pair of my sunglasses despite the rainy day.

After he leaves, I make coffee and suck down a cup, barely tasting it. Then I call Tullamore and talk to Allison. I end up telling her the bare bones of why I left work yesterday: I had a news alert set for the alias my abuser used years ago and saw an article saying he'd been arrested.

Hearing the struggle in my voice, she stops me and says she'll get my shifts covered for the next week.

"Lord knows you never go on vacation."

It's true. I have a ridiculous amount of Paid Time Off accrued, especially since it rolls over every year.

"Thanks, Allison. You're a good friend."

"Same, Soph. Be good to yourself this week, okay? Call me if you need anything—a shoulder to cry on, someone to eat an entire cake with. Or just someone to listen."

I thank her one more time and end the call before I start crying again. My eyes are puffy and tender, and my head is still pounding despite four ibuprofen.

Hours pass—enough of them that I know Matt is likely home. He's ignoring my calls. It hurts like a fucking hot poker in my chest, but I still don't blame him. I consider typing out an explanation and apology in a text message but eventually discard the idea. There's too much to say. Words that should be spoken face-to-face.

I force down a bowl of cereal. Make myself shower. Then I call Kelly, who in a stroke of luck isn't working today. She's at my apartment in thirty minutes.

We read the article and cry together. Then we open a bottle of wine and toast the law enforcement officers who brought him down. We toast the victims, too—past and present. There are more tears from both of us. I save the number of the FBI Victim Specialist, Nancy Faulkner, in my phone.

Just in case.

Over the course of the afternoon, we periodically order food, everything from donuts to Korean barbecue. We watch *The Godfather* and *Four Weddings and a Funeral.* Eventually, we pass out in my bed, our hands clasped in the space between us.

Other than a few check-in calls from Josh throughout the day, my phone doesn't ring.

I fall asleep with tears in my eyelashes, hope and regret on my tongue.

Sophie actually called twice last night. The first call came as Jackson, Nick, and I were leaving behind a craps table and a bunch of money. Disgruntled, tipsy, and tired from a day of golf, we'd just decided to head back to our rental house. I was on my phone ordering an Uber and declined her call.

I sent her a quick text, telling her I'd call as soon as we got to the house. And I did, but she didn't answer. I waited a bit and called again. No answer.

While Jackson and Nick made cocktails and headed for the hot tub in the backyard, I stretched out in bed and waited a few more minutes before trying her again. I'm not proud of how many times I called her between 11:00 p.m. and 3:00 a.m. Must have been close to twenty times.

At some point, Nick came in my room to find me pacing and losing my goddamn mind. He tried his best to talk me down, but he didn't understand, and I couldn't tell him *why* I was freaked the fuck out other than I was worried about Sophie. When he started insinuating that my reaction to not being able to reach her wasn't healthy, I almost punched him in the face.

Finally, at close to three in the morning, my phone rang.

She was drunk, slurring. Not making any sense at first. Then, for a brief minute, her voice grew eerily clear.

"I love you, Matthew Anders Sullivan. I didn't even know I could love someone like I love you, but I do. I love you so much I can't stand it sometimes. So much I feel like I'm going to burst with it.

"I'm sorry—so sorry… I wish I could be normal. I wish I didn't have this darkness inside me, suffocating me. I don't want you to drown too, okay?

"Maybe in another life, I'll be everything you need and we can have babies. Little blond babies with your smile. I'd really love that.

"Remember that, okay? Remember I love you."

Then she hung the fuck up. Like she hadn't just dropped a bomb and exploded my head.

Now, almost twenty-four hours later, I still haven't slept. My blood feels volcanic, but my skin is clammy and cold. I've been home since early this afternoon, but I can't seem to calm myself down.

She's called a few times, but I haven't called her back. I don't really know why, but I can't talk to her yet. I'm afraid of what I'll say.

I'm just... afraid.

My front door slams and two sets of footsteps come down the hallway, one heavy and one light.

I instantly regret calling them.

"What the actual fuck?" asks Julian as he and Rose round the corner.

Rose takes in my appearance—yesterday's clothes—and the disaster that is my kitchen. Then she calmly walks around her husband and starts closing all the cabinets.

"I was looking for something," I say, my voice shredded like I've been smoking cigarettes for thirty years. I was looking for a joint—which I have a habit of stashing in the kitchen—but I'm not about to tell my long-term sober best friend that.

Rose touches my back and I flinch. "Hey," she says softly. "You guys go sit down in the living room. I'll bring you something to eat and drink."

I follow Julian to the couch, then veer sharply away when an image of Sophie on the couch flashes in my mind. I collapse onto an armchair.

Julian brings me a blanket, tsking as he throws it over my legs. "You're shaking like a junkie. Why are you wearing shorts, bro?"

"It was seventy-four in Palm Springs," I say mutedly.

"Yeah, and you've been home for hours."

I can't meet his gaze. "I'm fucked-up. Mentally."

"Tell me something I don't know."

In spite of myself, my lips curve up on one side. "You're such a dick."

"Drink this," says Rose, sending Julian a glare before handing me a tumbler of what I know isn't water.

I give it a sniff, then wince. "Straight gin, really? That's nasty, Rosie Posie."

"I squirted some lime in it," she says flatly. "This is all you're getting to take the edge off, so drink up. Then you're eating a quesadilla and having a banana and a glass of milk. It'll settle your stomach. Oh, and I turned the heat on. It's a freezer in here, and that's saying something because I'm a literal furnace."

She sweeps out of the room, and Julian and I share a look.

"Pregnancy," he mouths.

It instantly reminds me of what Sophie said on the phone about little blond babies with my smile, how in another life, she'd want them.

In another life.

"Fucking hell," I mutter, then toss back the gin, grimacing as it leaves a trail of bitter heat down to my empty stomach. Twenty seconds later, I feel my heart rate finally slowing, though it probably has more to do with Julian and Rose than the booze.

A pan clatters onto the stove in the other room, and Rose strides back into the living room to look at me accusingly. "You have no tortillas. No cheddar. What is wrong with you?" She doesn't give me time to answer before pulling out her phone. "I'm ordering Mexican food."

Julian perks up. "Can I have—"

"You'll eat whatever I order," she says, giving him a smile so sweet she looks positively villainous.

To his credit, Julian just smiles back. "Sure. Sounds good." He pats the couch next to him, and she settles against his side, fingers flying over the screen of her phone.

I watch the interaction with fascination and a sour burst of longing. Eventually, Rose puts her phone down and looks from me to Julian and back to me.

Her eyes narrow. "I guess I'll rip off the Band-Aid,

then. Nick said you lost your shit last night because Sophie wasn't answering your calls."

I sink further into my chair. "It's not that simple."

"Obviously," she says softly. "Tell us what's going on, Matt. It won't leave this room."

"Consider us your emotional sponsors," adds Julian with a wry smile.

My hesitation isn't long. If it was anyone other than them sitting across from me, I wouldn't say anything at all. But Julian and Rose have fought their own battles—individually and together—with trauma. I trust them implicitly. And I need help.

So I tell them.

All of it.

When I finish, Julian brings me a glass of water and I suck it down, thanking him. Then he sits back down and rubs his temples. Rose stares thoughtfully at her lap.

Eventually, Julian breaks the silence. "Why *didn't* you call the police for a wellness check?" he asks, curious rather than admonishing.

I meet his dark gaze, reassured by the lack of judgment there. "Because even though her words were scary as fuck, I *know* her. She was crying—but not like she was saying goodbye. More like involuntary, giddy tears. Drunk sobs and hiccups. She even laughed a few times.

I don't know how else to explain it. If she'd been calm or sober…" A shudder wracks my body. "I would have called, no question."

Rose nods. "I understand completely." She releases a soft breath and grabs Julian's hand. "I think we can agree that Sophie had a rough night. We don't know why, or if there *was* a single reason. Given what she lived through, chances are it's something that's happened before and will happen again. That's something you're going to have to think about in the long run."

Julian nods. "She's right. It's obvious Sophie has come a long way from what happened to her, but it doesn't mean she doesn't carry demons. It might not be the best comparison, but I can relate a little. Just because I walked away from alcohol doesn't mean I'm not an alcoholic. I always have the potential to fall back off the cliff into old behaviors and coping mechanisms."

I swallow hard, looking down at my lap.

"If you want a future with her," continues Rose gently, "you're going to have to realize her past will always be with her. You have to accept it. If you can't do that, Matt, you need to let her go."

Everything in me revolts at the notion. Rose sees the emotions playing out on my face and smiles softly.

Julian hugs her to him, telling me, "I suggest you educate yourself on how to best support her. Understand what happens to her physically and mentally. The longterm effects of her trauma that she'll deal with her entire life."

"I've been trying," I say haltingly. "But I think you're right. I don't really understand what it's like for her day-to-day. When I actually think about it, my brain kind of overloads. It makes me angry, sad, grateful... I-I think she's a fucking miracle."

"She is," Rose whispers.

"What stopped you from reaching out to her when you got home?" asks Julian.

I shake my head helplessly. "I don't know. I *want* to talk to her. But I also need to get my head straight. I'm still angry at her. I know it's stupid. Unfair. I wish I weren't."

Julian stirs. "At the heart of anger—"

"Is fear," I finish, rolling my eyes. "Yeah, I know, Obi Wan Ashburn."

He laughs. "Fuck you."

The doorbell rings. Rose's eyes light up. "That's the food. I'm starving."

Julian stands, giving his wife an affectionate smile. "Be right back."

When he's gone, Rose says pointedly, "Don't give up on her, Mattie," and I know she's thinking about how Julian didn't give up on her while she was working through crazy shit from her own past.

"I won't," I tell her.

An hour later, when they're gone, I finally shower and change into warmer clothes. Back downstairs, I slump into the armchair again and stare at my phone.

Sophie stopped calling a few hours ago, and my heart hurts thinking about what she may be feeling. Like I'm rejecting her. Like I don't love her.

Just hang on, Dollface.

I lift the phone and listen as it rings.

"Matt?" The voice is surprised. A little wary.

I take a breath. "Hey, Josh. I need your help."

30

The skies above Alki Beach are a clear, icy blue. Overhead, the sun is pale and glittering, and the frigid air makes every breath a small cloud.

Though I sit on a blanket in a little pocket of solitude, I'm not alone. Couples and singles walk dogs, jog the coastline, or linger with their faces lifted upward in worship of Vitamin D.

I check my watch again, wondering where Josh is. The coffee I bought him is cold; mine is long gone. My nose is numb and running, and despite thick wool socks and boots, my toes are ice cubes.

I'm about to pull out my phone and text my brother when I spy someone approaching from the corner of my eye.

It's not Josh.

My heart jackknifes and ejects all the longing it's stored up over the last two days. I drink in the sight of him: a beanie pulled over his ears, blond hair sticking out in tufts. Eyes that match both the water and sky. Thick coat, jeans, and boots. A nervous expression on his face.

"Hey, Dollface."

"Hi," I whisper.

His gaze flickers over me. "Can I sit?"

I nod, swallowing hard against the coffee that wants to come back up. "I take it Josh isn't coming?"

A small smile plays on his lips as he shakes his head. I scoot over to make room on the blanket, my heart bouncing around my chest, my thoughts pinwheeling. He settles beside me. I close my eyes, fighting the desire to throw myself into his arms and sob.

"I'm sorry," I say finally, staring at the ocean so I don't have to see his face. "I know I scared you. I don't blame you for wanting space the last few days. And I-I understand if you want, if you don't want—" I cut off abruptly, incapable of finishing the sentence, of speaking what I dread the most.

"I hear you," he says after a moment, "but you don't owe me an apology. I owe *you* one. I panicked. I let fear control me. And I didn't support you when you needed me to."

I turn fast toward him, my eyes wide with surprise and dismay. "No, Matt. This isn't your fault."

"Sophie," he says, his eyes steady and clear, his voice so gentle I want to weep. "Josh told me about the article. About what happened after—the blackout and flashbacks. You *do not* need to apologize to me."

All I can do is stare at him as he continues. "I've spent the last couple of days learning about PTSD and assault survivors, reading and watching videos, basically scouring everything the internet has to offer. I ordered like ten books that should be here in the next few days." He smiles slightly. "Josh probably wants to throat-punch me after how many times I've called him with questions."

"Matt," I choke out.

Expression morphing in distress, he shifts closer to me, a hand lifting, then stalling near my face. "Baby, don't cry." His own eyes redden, which only makes my tears come faster. "Can I touch you?"

I nod and sob, "Yes."

Then his arms are around me, solid and comforting and real, pulling my broken pieces together, melting and sealing them into a new whole.

"I love you," I gasp into his chest, then lift my head and look into his teary eyes. "I'm in love with you, Matthew."

He grins. "I know. You told me a bunch of times."

I groan. "I was so drunk. God, what else did I say?"

"Besides the dark shit I'd rather never think about again?"

I wince. "Yeah."

His smile sharpens. "You love me so much you can't stand it sometimes. It makes you feel like you're going to burst. And you want to have my babies. Little blond babies with my smile."

My jaw drops. "Shut up."

He laughs. "Don't worry, I won't hold you to it."

I smile, and it feels like the first real one in days. "What if I want you to? Someday, I mean."

He freezes, eyes widening. His mouth opens, closes, and he finally says, "I don't know when I fell in love with you. Sometimes it feels like it happened in stages, and other times I think I was a goner the moment you told me you fall asleep getting tattooed. Or when I realized you'd drawn the art on my back. Maybe Josh laid the groundwork for years with all his stories. I've always been intrigued." He shakes his head, eyes never leaving mine. "I can't explain it, but it feels like I've always loved you. Like I've always known you even though I hadn't found you yet. And even if this road is bumpy sometimes, there's no one else I want to be on it with. I'm yours—Mmf."

My lips smother the rest of his words.

31

"*I*s this okay?"

"Matt, I'm going to smack you if you ask me that one more time."

His forehead drops to mine. "I'm sorry."

Huffing in frustration, I push him off me, yanking my shirt down and zipping my jeans back up. Hilarity, annoyance, and rising despair slosh inside me as I sit up and gaze down at him. Lower lip caught in his teeth, his blue eyes are tortured. Uncertain. Fearful. Apologetic.

"We need more time," I say weakly. "We can't force this."

He covers his face with his hands, emitting a low, disgruntled groan. My eyes trail down his body and snag on the evidence—or rather, the blatant lack thereof—of our third attempt at having sex since the beach on Sunday.

"I'm gonna go." My voice cracks. Embarrassed and near tears, I scoot off the bed and head for the door.

"Sophie, wait."

Already halfway across his bedroom, I turn and force myself to meet his gaze. I speak before he can—I can't handle hearing another apology right now.

"It's okay, Matt. This is a lot for anyone to deal with. I didn't want—" I swallow hard, struggling for calm. "This is part of why I've never been in a serious relationship, and why I wish... things were different."

"I love you," he whispers.

"I know," I say, nodding bravely. "I love you, too. But I also know that trauma spills into the lives of people who care about the survivors."

"We'll get through this."

Will we?

I don't know. We've had a lot of hard conversations the last few days. Conversations I never want to have with anyone again. Intimate, uncomfortable, raw. He hasn't asked me for the gruesome details, thank God— and I'd never tell him any, even if he did—but he's read enough and in this case, imagination is poison.

Having fully confronted and processed what I went through, now when he touches me—*wants me*—he can't separate his lust from what was done to me and is invariably crippled by shame.

Because he's a good man.

"I know," I tell him, wishing I believed it. "Call me before you go to sleep?"

He looks like he wants to say something else but wisely swallows it back. "Okay. Drive safe."

It isn't until I'm opening the door of my apartment that I realize we didn't kiss goodbye.

THE FOLLOWING MORNING, I wake up with the singular drive to get out of my head and away from everything that reminds me of Matt.

At 10:00 a.m., I show up at Beka's high school with the excuse of a fake doctor's appointment. I haven't busted her out in a few years, but she remembers the game, showing up in the office with just the right amount of pouting and feet-dragging.

We're giggling by the time we get to my car, where I hand her a hot chocolate.

She takes a sip, then grins at me. "Best day ever. You saved me from a pop quiz in English."

My smile freezes. "Shit. Don't tell Mom."

She laughs. "Don't worry. I'll make it up tomorrow—

after I actually read the last chapters of *The Great Gatsby*."

"Okay, good." I turn on the car and nod at her seat belt, which she puts on. "What do you want to do?"

She shrugs, her eyes alight with happiness. "Whatever you want. I'm down for anything. Hanging at your apartment, seeing a movie, getting food."

"Mani/pedis, then shopping," I say decisively.

Beka squeals. "Yes!"

We get matching polish on both fingers and toes—a maroon so dark it looks black—then have lunch and head to the mall for retail therapy. Beka is her usual bubbly, erratic self, talking nonstop and jumping between topics so fast my head spins.

The day is perfect until we're walking back to my car around 4:00 p.m., arms laden with bags. My credit card hates me, but I can't regret a single purchase.

When we reach the row where I parked, Beka says, "Hang on a sec, Soph."

I pause, turning right as she sags against the trunk of a sedan. "Beks!" Dropping my bags, I rush to her side.

She scowls at me, pushing me away weakly when I reach for her. Her face is chalk-white under the fading light of the cloudless afternoon sky.

"Stop. Just need to... catch my breath."

Ignoring her feeble attempt to bat my hand away, I

grab her wrist and lift her smartwatch. The face flashes with a warning that makes my blood freeze in my veins.

Low Heart Rate.

Leaving our bags scattered over the asphalt, I slip my arm under hers and walk her to the nearest island where a bare-branched tree lists. Guiding her down to the curb, I sit beside her and lift her wrist again, waiting to see if her heart rate comes back up.

Instead, it dips again, and this time the watch starts vibrating.

"Hey, are you guys okay?"

I barely hear the bystander as I scramble for my phone, yanking it out of my jacket pocket and dialing 911. Beka sags heavily against my side. I grab her, holding her up, and almost drop my phone.

"Beka!" I seize her jaw, tilting her face up to see that she's lost consciousness.

"Nine-one-one—what's your emergency?"

"We need an ambulance! My sister passed out. She has heart defects and her heart rate just dipped to forty-four! Please, please hurry!" I tell her the name of the mall and the department store entrance behind us.

"Paramedics are on the way. Stay with me on the line until they reach you."

I put the phone on speaker and drop it to the ground. I don't hear anything else the woman says, but she keeps talking and somehow, I keep answering her questions. A crowd has formed around us. Someone collects our shopping bags and puts them on the ground next to us.

My world narrows to my sister, the pulse on the wrist my fingers are jammed into, the corresponding number on her watch, and the breath that hits my neck where I've tucked her head.

The sound of sirens grows louder, then cuts off as the ambulance pulls into the parking lot. The crowd scatters to make way for the vehicle. In seconds, a man and a woman in uniform appear before me. The woman puts two fingers to Beka's neck and fires questions at me. I give her the rundown of her heart defects and ongoing monitoring, as well as her two heart surgeries and what just happened.

Beka stirs with a confused moan.

Tears finally spill from my eyes, held back the last minutes by sheer force of will. "It's okay, Beks," I murmur, stroking her back. "I'm here. You passed out. We're gonna take a ride to the hospital."

"No," she whines.

The male paramedic gently extricates her from my arms, picking her up and carrying her to a stretcher. I scramble to my feet, grabbing my purse and phone, and follow. After Beka's loaded into the ambulance, I climb up and perch on the bench to clasp her cool hand.

As the paramedic places electrodes on her chest attached to a heart monitor, a good samaritan shoves our shopping bags on the floor inside the door. "Thank you," I whisper. They nod and disappear.

Beka's rolling eyes find mine as the doors close. She's still too pale, but her watch isn't vibrating anymore and the monitor has started reading. I see her heart rate come up to sixty, then sixty-four, seventy…

I release a slow, shuddering breath.

"Good, that's good," murmurs the paramedic, flashing us both a reassuring smile.

The driver's door slams, and we start moving. As soon as we hit the main road, the siren comes on and we accelerate.

"God, I hate this," mutters Beka, glancing surreptitiously at the gorgeous man currently watching the monitor. I'm relieved to see her cheeks actually flushing with embarrassment.

A slightly unhinged laugh comes from my chest. "What? This is awesome. Super hot paramedics rescuing you? Splitting traffic like a boss? Come on. Best day ever."

The man chuckles as Beka shoots daggers at me from her eyeballs. "I hate you," she mouths.

I laugh as tears stream down my face.

We're at the hospital minutes later. Beka is rolled into the building—one hand over her face in utter mortification—and I trail behind to call my mom and Josh. They have eerily similar reactions to the news: both are preternaturally calm and inform me they're on their way. Then I send a quick text to Matt, telling him what happened and where I am before tucking my phone away.

The paramedics transfer Beka to a bed, simultaneously updating the nurse who followed us into the room. Then they're on their way out, back to saving lives on the streets.

The handsome one gives Beka a wink before he leaves, which makes my sister turn beet red. "Kill me now," she hisses at me.

Fifteen minutes later, Mom, Josh, and Patrick arrive right as the doctor appears. And thirty minutes after that, I walk wearily into the waiting room for a breather.

As soon as I push through the doors, I stop and stare. Then I start crying again, though this time what I feel is relief. Vast, warm, melting relief.

Matt's arms come around me, forming a barrier between me and the world. I mumble into his sweatshirt, "I've cried more in the last few weeks than I have in seven years. I'm getting sick of it."

He kisses my temple. "Come on, let's get some fresh air."

Tucked under his arm, I let him draw me outside and away from the bustling entrance of the ER. He hugs me tightly until I finally feel the knot of fear inside me relax, then he lifts my face, wiping tears from my cheeks.

"How's she doing?" he asks softly.

I take a trembling breath. "She's okay right now. The doctor ordered a bunch of tests. Beka admitted she's been having symptoms for the last week—episodes of dizziness, shortness of breath, fatigue. She told our mom, but Mom didn't tell Josh and me. She called Beka's cardiologist over the weekend and was waiting for a call back."

"She wanted to protect you," Matt murmurs.

I nod. "Yeah, plus Beka admitted she downplayed what she was feeling when she told my mom." I stare blindly at a nearby tree. "I keep thinking about what would have happened if I hadn't pulled her from school today. If she'd been off campus with friends for lunch, or on the bus home—"

"But you were there," he says, thumb sweeping across my jaw. "You were right there, and she's okay."

I take a deep breath and nod. "Her cardiologist is at this hospital, too, so he's on his way." I pause, swallowing the knot in my throat. "We always knew this was a possibility—her condition getting worse. She's been fine for so long, I guess I forgot what this particular kind of fear feels like."

"What does 'worse' mean?" he asks carefully.

"Best-case scenario, she'll need a pacemaker. Worst-case scenario, another heart surgery. We'll know more after the tests."

He hugs me to him again. "What do you need?"

"You," I whisper. "Just you. Thank you for being here."

"Of course," he murmurs. "I'm here for you. Always. I'll stay as long as you need."

I lift my face and his lips cover mine. The kiss is gentle. Soft and warm. And for a few seconds, no fear can touch me.

eka has surgery the next day to place a pacemaker and defibrillator in her abdomen. In the hours leading up to it, she acts like a total asshole to everyone, but we know it's because she's scared. We're all scared, even though the doctors assure us several times that it's a relatively simple surgery and there's a good chance she'll be able to go home in twenty-four hours.

To everyone's relief—and my mom's near meltdown—she comes through surgery with no issues. Once she's in recovery and resting comfortably, Mom insists Josh, Patrick, and I go home and sleep. We don't put up much of a fight, all of us virtually zombies.

Once Patrick is dropped off, Josh takes me home. I smile tiredly when I see my car in the parking lot outside my building—Matt and Julian retrieved it from the mall and drove it home for me.

I mumble a goodbye to Josh and drag myself inside. The elevator is halfway to my floor when I realize I forgot to pull my apartment key off of my key ring, which Matt has because he drove my car home.

"Shit on a stick," I grumble, pulling out my phone.

He picks up on the first ring. "Hi, Dollface."

"You didn't hide my front door key under the mat by chance, did you?"

"Nope," he says lightly. "But I did head over here when you texted me you were leaving the hospital. Pickle and I are reheating Chicken Tortilla Soup for you."

Tears of exhaustion and stress and sheer, unadulterated happiness spring to my eyes. "Shut the fuck up. Really?"

He laughs softly.

The elevator doors open. I step into the hallway, and a second later my apartment door opens. A smiling Matt pokes his head out.

In that moment, I know he's it. Mine. Right in front of me is a love I never believed possible, and I'll do whatever is necessary to keep him.

However messy life gets, however hard, I'm never letting this man go.

FLOATING SOMEWHERE between sleep and waking, I snuggle closer to Matt, close enough my lips graze his throat. He's asleep, but his arm tightens reflexively around me and he sighs.

We're both clothed, wearing T-shirts and boxers. Far too many barriers, in my opinion. He's a furnace of heat and virility against me, his legs scissored with mine, my breasts compressed against his chest. I shift a little until his thigh brushes between my legs, and a small sound escapes me. He stirs with a sleepy rumble of contentment.

I need him. Right now.

My hips rock forward of their own accord, and his hand floats up my spine, fingers closing possessively around the back of my neck. He swells against my stomach, thickening and hardening, and releases a shaky breath against my hair.

"Sophie," he whispers, raw and full of longing.

I push him onto his back, whipping off my shirt in the same movement. His eyes blink open, the haze in them clearing as he takes me in. When he opens his mouth, I put a finger to his lips and shake my head. His gaze sharpens, flickering down to my breasts. I see the moment he surrenders—chest lifting in a deep breath as his need for me eclipses everything else.

I draw his shirt up, exposing his mouthwatering torso, riddled with art and sharp delineations of muscle. I kiss every tattoo. Lick and tug at his nipples with my teeth until he growls. The sound reverberates between my legs, but for now, I ignore my own need. I want him to know how much I adore him—what he means to me. How much I want his pleasure.

Slithering down his body, I drag the waistband of his boxers over his erection, freeing him for my hand. My mouth follows. I take him as deep as I can, licking my way down, then sucking hard as I retreat. Then I do it again, preening as his breath hitches, as his hands come up to cradle my face and neck.

"Oh, fuck, that feels so good." His whisper is harsh, the words making the ache between my legs almost unbearable. "Are you dripping for me, Dollface?"

I hum around him, then slap his hand as he reaches for my boxers. He groans, giving in to my demand to stay in charge, and his hips start thrusting gently into my mouth. Heady satisfaction fills me and I devote myself to making him fall apart.

Gentle fingers push hair back from my face. I look up to see him watching me, features tight, eyes glittering with carnal demand. His jaw clenches and he licks his lips. "You want me to come in your mouth, baby?"

I nod, and the savage look on his face makes wetness drip down my thighs. His grip on my hair intensifies, his body stiffening, and he whispers my name as he spills down my throat.

I barely have a second to gloat before he drags me up his body and covers my mouth with his, tongue claiming every crevasse like he's hunting his own flavor. I've never been more aroused in my life... until he tosses me to the bed and tears off my shorts, then buries his head between my legs.

I arch off the bed with a cry, my hands flailing until I find his hair. Then I hold on as he devours me like I'm his last meal.

My orgasm comes embarrassingly fast, a bright jolt to my system. I'm still twitching when he slides inside me in a single, smooth thrust. He covers me with his body, biceps bracketing my head, and his tongue dives into my mouth in a wet, sinful kiss. His hips swirl with slow, devastating intent, and another, deeper sensation quickens inside me.

"I love you," he whispers between kisses. "I want this. *You*. Forever. Be mine forever, Sophie."

There's only one thing to say, so I say it.

"I'm yours forever."

33

"When did you buy this house?" I ask, trying to sound nonchalant as I follow Matt into his kitchen with groceries.

His brows arch with surprise, then he frowns thoughtfully. "I think it's been almost a year now. Crazy. It doesn't feel like that long."

"Ah, that's cool."

He gives me a little grin. "What's going on in that head?"

"Nothing. I was just curious."

I avoid his eyes as I start unpacking groceries for tonight's Christmas Eve dinner. Another tradition of the band, and Matt's hosting this year.

As fun as it sounded, I wasn't going to come. I haven't spent a Christmas Eve away from my family in my lifetime. But Mom and Josh basically uninvited me, and Beka—who's recovering well but has been a moody nightmare about missing school last week—told me I was being stupid and that if I didn't go she'd disown me. Brat.

At least I'll see them tomorrow. Matt and I decided on breakfast with my family and dinner with his. It's all very domestic and serious-relationshippy, and I'm avoiding thinking about it all because a part of me is continuously in a low-key freakout.

Not that we've talked about moving in together, or anything about the future at all since he asked to keep me forever, but I have this amorphous anxiety I can't quit. Like any second it's all going to blow up in my face, which only makes me want to grasp onto what's happening harder... which in turn triggered a line of thinking when I walked into the house about how long Melody lived here with him, if she chose any of the decor or left anything behind, and whether he wants me to move in with him at all, and how Pickle would adjust, and...

"Whoa, Dollface." Warm hands frame my face. "Breathe with me. In—two, three four. Hold. Out—two three four. There we go." When oxygen returns to my brain and I smile weakly, he kisses my forehead. "What's up?"

"Sorry," I choke out, then shake my head. "Just had a little meltdown. I'm fine."

"Okay." He gives me a soft, sweet kiss and returns to unpacking groceries.

I watch him for a few moments, restless and fidgety, until I finally blurt, "Did you buy this house with Melody?"

He stills, then lowers a head of lettuce and turns, his expression neutral. "No," he answers, then clears his throat and drags a hand through his hair. "We were renting and I... I bought this house as a surprise for her after we got engaged." A wry smile curls his lips. "She hated it."

I gape. "What? That's insane. This house is fucking gorgeous."

Features sharpening, he nods. "Yeah, I love it, too. But I think I bought it for the wrong person."

His meaning is unmistakable, and the air leaves my lungs in a rush even as blood surges to my head. He stalks toward me and lifts my face with a knuckle under my chin.

"I know that's hard for you to hear," he says gently, a thumb brushing across my lower lip. "Here's the thing, Sophie. I've accepted that it will take time for you to trust me completely—to trust this—and I'm okay with that. But you need to know that I'll never stop loving you this way. I'll never stop showing you and telling you how I feel about you. And one day, you're going to believe it."

He catches a tear as it escapes the corner of my eye, then dips his head to kiss me. "Now grab an apron because I'm putting you to work." His head lifts, a sparkle in his eye. "Wait—you *can* peel an apple, right?"

A laugh bursts out of me and I shove him, which is basically like pushing a wall. "Fuck off."

He chuckles and grabs an apron from a hook on the wall, tossing it at my face. We spend the next hour prepping our agreed-upon dishes—scalloped potatoes, green beans, and apple pie—which means Matt basically orders me around because, as my brother is so fond of reminding me, I can't cook worth shit. Matt, on the other hand, is all confidence.

Nick and Kat arrive around noon with a giant hunk of prime rib, and within ten minutes, Kat and I are booted from the kitchen. Neither of us is put out by the fact, and we happily take glasses of wine to the living room. By the time Julian, Rose, Jackson, and Christina— who seems to be sticking around—arrive with more sides, Kat and I are halfway through *National Lampoon's Christmas Vacation* and the smells coming from the kitchen are mouthwatering.

"You guys have the right idea," says Rose, grinning as

she sits next to us, a hand curled lovingly over her growing belly.

"I learned the lesson early on," Kat drawls. "They're partners on stage, but competitors in the kitchen. It's best to stay as far away as possible and reap the benefits."

I laugh, remembering how intense Matt was earlier about the potatoes being scalloped *just so.*

Christina walks into the room, a nervous smile on her face. She lingers near the couch, gaze flickering toward the three of us before fixing on the television.

I know what social awkwardness looks and feels like, so I say, "Come sit down, Christina. This couch is like eight feet long."

She gives me a grateful smile, but still seems tense when she sits on the other side of me. I feel her gaze on my face. "Thanks for having me today, Sophie."

I look at her in confusion. "Uh, you're welcome?"

Kat whispers out of the corner of her mouth, "She thinks you live here."

"Oh." I laugh and feel myself blush as I tell Christina, "Matt and I aren't living together, but I'll be sure to pass along the thanks to him."

"You aren't?" Christina asks, her eyes studying me a bit too intently. Even the wine in my system doesn't dilute a twinge of unease.

Before I can process the odd moment, Nick's boisterous voice fills the room. "Ladies! It's that time again—the race is upon us! You have one minute to get to the starting line. Last two in the pool are on dish duty!"

Having been warned in advance by Matt, I only groan a little as I get to my feet. About the last thing I want to do right now is leave the cozy, warm house to jump into the freezing cold pool, but there's also a part of me that's thrilled to be included in this weird-as-hell Christmas Eve tradition.

Christina's the first to scurry from the room. She passes Julian as he enters and drops to the couch beside Rose. At my questioning look, he shrugs. "I'd rather hang with preggers here, and I don't mind doing dishes."

"Dammit," mutters Kat as she stands and pulls off her sweater and shirt, revealing a one-piece bathing suit. She glowers at Rose. "Lucky bitch."

Rose laughs and lifts her glass of sparkling water. "You could always get yourself knocked up."

Kat makes a face, then slips off her leggings, picks up her clothes, and tosses them on an armchair. Nick reappears with an appreciative whistle for his wife. He crosses in long strides and picks her up, dropping her like a sack over his shoulder. Kat squeals in outrage, but Nick just cackles as he carts her from the room.

Matt's voice summons me from the hallway, "Come on, Dollface!"

"Have fun." Rose laughs as I hightail it from the room.

WHEN THE LAST couple has left, and the last dish is put away, Matt and I collapse onto the couch. I rub my cheek against his chest and he hums in contentment, his arms curling around me.

"I can't believe you betrayed me like that," he mumbles with warm humor. "We were supposed to be a team and take out the competition."

I giggle. "I was just following the rules of the race: every man and woman for themselves. Can't blame me if I had natural allies."

I grin as I remember the look on Matt's face as I'd ditched my drawstring pants and sweater and run past him out the back door, leaving him scrambling to catch up. Then his absolute shock when Nick—dripping wet from his winning jump—had viciously yanked his swim trunks to his ankles. Suffice to say, by the time Matt made it into the water, he was dead last.

"Why did you even jump in?" I ask, laughing as I look up at him.

He considers the question, then shrugs. "Habit?"

I shake my head affectionately. "You're so weird." A giant yawn cracks my jaw. "We should go to sleep. Tomorrow's going to be crazy."

He tilts my face up and gives me a soft kiss. "I want to give you one of your Christmas presents now."

"Pfft. Sacrilege. Plus, we agreed on one gift!"

He chuckles and shifts, pulling something from his pocket. "It's nothing big. Doesn't even count. See?"

I stare at the silver key in his fingers. Sitting up, I look from it to his grinning face. "Is that...?"

"Yes, it's a house key. You already know the alarm code." When I just stare at him, he plants a hand on the back of my head and pulls me in for a smacking kiss. "It's just a key, Sophie. So you can come here whenever you want, for anything, whether I'm here or not. There's no expectation attached." He smiles knowingly. "You have another month or two before I ask you to move in with me."

"What?" I squeak.

His smile sharpens. "By my take, we've been together for four and a half months." I open my mouth, but he presses a finger to my lips. "Our first date was bowling. A blind date, if you will. No arguing, Dollface, you know as well as I do that it's true—this was inevitable from the beginning. You're made for me, and

I'm made for you. We just took a longer route to get here than most. It may seem fast on paper, but I've been waiting for you my whole life."

This time, when I open my mouth, he seizes it with his in a deep, melting kiss. My blood tingles and my bones melt as he kisses his way across my jaw and down my neck.

"I wish I weren't so tired," he mumbles.

On cue, I yawn. He laughs, and we make it off the couch and upstairs to bed, listlessly brushing our teeth before stripping and climbing into bed.

I drift toward sleep with his heartbeat beneath my ear, a pervasive calm radiating through me. I can almost feel the darkness inside me curling inward, shrinking and sinking like a rock in water, down and down.

It will always be a part of me, and I know I'll feel it again, but never with the same intensity I have in the past. The darkness did its job protecting me, but it's not alone anymore.

Love is more powerful than darkness, anyway.

34

"*How's Beka doing? How was Christmas? Tell me everything.*"

I laugh as I lean against the doorframe of Allison's office, having just dropped my purse off in my own. We've barely had a second to talk in the madness of the last four days. Between a post-Christmas rush like we've never seen, people calling out sick, and the scramble to get coverage, we've been working our asses off, both pulling massive overtime.

"Beka's doing great. Adjusting surprisingly well. Christmas was good." At her searching look, I add, "Really good."

A wide smile takes over her face. "I'm so glad."

My cheeks flush as I remember Christmas morning, which Matt and I spent the early hours of naked in bed. After we'd showered and made coffee, we unwrapped our gifts to each other, only one as per my demand. Matt even agreed to stick to my fifty-dollar price limit.

I gave him the original art of my back piece, reframed in much nicer wood and now safe behind glass. It wasn't a hard gift, as he's been begging me for it for weeks. His excitement was palpable, and he'd immediately found a hammer and nail and hung it right by his bed while I watched in a happy stupor.

Then he gave me a single box filled with the most random and perfect assortment of things, smugly informing me that he *technically* followed the one-gift rule. I let it slide because inside I found my favorite toiletries to keep at his house, bags of my favorite candies, a pair of socks with Pickle's face plastered all over the fabric, my favorite candle, and finally, a lumpy wooden carving roughly shaped in a sphere, about the size of my palm.

"It's a Weeping Buddha," he told me softly. "Story goes, this version of the Buddha surrendered to suffering in order to carry our pain for us. When you're overwhelmed, you can hold him and give your suffering to him."

Allison's giggle snaps me back to the present. "You're

so in love. If it was anyone else in front of me right now, I'd say it's disgusting."

I blush harder. "Har har. How was your Christmas?"

"Amazing, tha—"

"Hey, bosses, we're slammed out here," Grey says breathlessly from behind me.

The next hours are a blur of customers. Things don't calm down until after three, but most of the tables in the café are still full, and though the line is short, it's never empty.

I'm manning the registers with Dania while Allison handles drink orders and Grey delivers sandwiches, salads, and soups from the kitchen.

In the four-second break between customers, Dania asks me, "Any plans for New Year's?"

I open my mouth to answer, but my next customer does it for me. "You're coming to the party, right? With Matt?" Christina grins at me from across the counter. She's alone, looking put together as always in a full face of makeup, her blond hair curled beneath a fuzzy beanie.

I smile back. "Hey! Yeah, we'll be there."

"Good," she says, smile staying fixed as she looks over my head at the giant chalkboard with menu and drink options.

"Is this your first time at Tullamore?" I ask.

She nods, eyes flickering down to me. "I'll have a small latte with nonfat milk, please."

"You got it." I pull the cup and write the order on it, then slide it onto the counter toward the drink station. "Anything to eat?"

She laughs. "God no, I won't be able to fit into my dress tomorrow."

Dania makes a faint gagging noise beside me. I barely manage to keep my face blank. "Okay, then." I give her the total for her drink, then turn my screen around so she can swipe her card.

"Thanks, Sophie," she says with a smile. "See you tomorrow." She heads for the pickup counter, her perfume trailing behind her. I watch her go, frowning, the same odd feeling from Christmas Eve making my senses prickle.

"You're friends with her?" murmurs Dania.

I glance at her. "Sort of? I don't know her well, but she's always been nice to me." At Dania's confused expression, I add, "She's dating one of my boyfriend's best friends."

She gasps. "Who are you? Did I just hear the B-word come out of your mouth?"

I laugh at her feigned horror. "Yeah, you did."

The customers keep coming, and we keep working with barely a pause until Dania gleefully pulls the doors closed and Grey switches off the illuminated Open sign.

I let them take a breather and haggle over the playlist while I start the closing routine at the registers.

An hour and a half later, I unlock my apartment to the familiar meows of Pickle and the warm, welcome arms of Matt. I don't need to tell him how exhausted I am; he just guides me into the bathroom and draws me a bath, massaging my stiff shoulders until I'm boneless. Once the bath is full and a candle is lit, he strips off my clothes. He even ties my hair into a messy bun on top of my head.

As I sink into the hot water that smells like lavender, my eyes close in utter bliss. "What did I do to deserve you?"

His lips press briefly to my forehead. "All you've ever had to do was be yourself. Be right back."

He returns with a glass of ice water and apple slices, then sits against the wall next to the tub. When I gape at him, he rolls his eyes playfully and feeds me an apple slice.

"You've never had someone take care of you before, have you?"

I finish chewing, then take a sip of the ice water he hands me. "Not like this, no."

A smile flirts with his lips. "Makes you feel uncomfortable as fuck, huh?"

I nod slowly. "It's... a bit like slipping into another dimension. In a good way," I add quickly.

Matt's eyes are steady on mine as he reads me like a book. "I'm in this for the long haul, Sophie. I love you like I've never loved anything or anyone."

I want to grimace, to deflect, but instead I force myself to *hear it* and *feel it*. I study his face, the face I've drawn a thousand times, the one I fantasized about for years before he bulldozed into my life with his unfailing goodness, wicked humor, and disarming honesty.

As I watch, mischief sparks in his eyes. "I'd ask you to marry me tomorrow if I didn't think you'd lose your shit."

My heart slingshots into my ribs and I sit up fast, my foot slipping off the side of the tub. Water sloshes over the rim, splashing Pickle, who mewls and darts out the door.

Matt tsks, shaking his head. "Poor Pickle." Face the picture of innocence, he pops an apple slice into my open mouth. "Chew, Dollface."

I do, a little surprised when I don't choke. "You can't say shit like that," I finally say.

"Why?" he asks, head tilted and eyes level on my face. "And don't say it's confusing. It's the opposite of confusing. I'm making my intentions clear. I'm keeping you, Sophie Marshall."

He sets down the plate of apple slices and leans forward. I sit frozen, still reeling as his cheek grazes mine. His mouth drags to my ear.

"I'm. Keeping. You," he whispers, words punctuated by little nips along my earlobe. "Now get out of the bath and sit on my face. I've been waiting hours for dessert."

’m actually surprised Matt lets me out of his house in the dress I’m wearing. It’s one of Kelly’s, a shimmering silver sheath that’s nearly obscene thanks to her being four inches shorter than me.

Not that we’ll be in public or in front of cameras. The party Christina alluded to is at Julian and Rose’s house in Edmonds, which is basically a private compound.

Halfway there, Matt breaks.

“At least tell me you put on underwear,” he growls, hot gaze flashing to my legs, adorned only in tattoos and moisturizer that makes my skin gleam. “Christ, Dollface, it’s going to be a miracle if I don’t beat the shit out of every dude who looks at you.”

I immediately feel a spike of regret. “I can change,” I

say quickly. "Just turn around. We'll be late, but whatever."

"No, no," he says, blowing out a breath. "I'd be a hypocrite if I made you change. Here I am, asking you to be with me and deal with my... life."

I immediately remember all the women who'd plastered themselves on him at the meet-and-greet. "Yeah. Can't say I'll ever get used to random women pawing you." I reach out and squeeze his hand. "But I trust you, and I accept it if it means I have you."

He draws my hand to his mouth, planting a kiss on my knuckles that I feel an echo of between my legs. Chasing the sensation is a vivid recall of forty minutes ago, when he'd first seen me in the dress and immediately fallen to his knees, yanking up the fabric and spreading me open for his tongue.

"You're off tomorrow, right?" he asks.

"Yes," I confirm. "Allison and I trade off, and I worked last year."

"Good," he says shortly. "Fair warning: you're spending the day naked."

I'm still smiling—purring, really—when we drive through the gates of Rose and Julian's house and up the winding driveway. Even though Matt warned me, I'm daunted by the number of cars and, once we get inside, the number of people.

Matt's hand secure in mine, we wander through the crowds, stopping often as people call out greetings. I'm introduced over and over again, and while I never get sick of Matt telling people I'm his girlfriend, I forget most names the second they're spoken.

Eventually, we find familiar faces in the spacious downstairs game room, where Julian and Rose are cuddling on a couch. On the other side of the room, Nick and Jackson sink balls on a pool table, the area dense with heckling spectators. Not far from that crowd is another. I spot Kat's red hair as she throws a dart at a target on the wall and hits the bull's-eye. She squeals in delight and yells, "Pay up!" to her unlucky competition.

Once I'm safely seated next to Rose, Matt gives me a kiss and goes in search of drinks.

"Happy New Year," I tell Rose, who smiles warmly at me.

"Same to you, Sophie." She bumps my shoulder with hers. "Have I mentioned how glad I am that I was so wrong about you and Matt?"

I blush. "Ha, no."

Her smile softens, dark eyes lucid and full of quiet contentment. "I'm so happy for my brother-from-another-mother. And for you."

Julian throws me a smile. "Me too." A second later, he says, "Rose," in a low tone that makes both Rose and me stiffen. I lean forward to see him staring at the hallway.

All I see are strangers chatting or passing by. Then someone moves and I see Christina and another woman, a brunette in a tiny blue dress whose face is turned away. Christina whispers something. The woman nods and they disappear down the hallway.

Rose snarls, "What the fuck?" in a tone I've never heard from her. Her head whips toward Julian, long curls almost smacking me in the face. "Help me up, will you?"

Julian, already halfway off the couch, looks down on his wife with immeasurable patience. "You will not be throwing punches at almost four months pregnant. I've got it." He leans back down to kiss her cheek.

"Get her the hell out of here," Rose hisses fiercely.

Julian nods, gives me an unreadable look, and strides through the crowd, which parts for him because... well, he's Julian Ashburn.

Rose sinks back onto the couch. A couple of men approach the open section, but Rose scowls at them until they veer away.

I force a laugh. "Does Julian need backup?"

"Nah. Stay with me. He'll take care of it."

Something in her voice sets off alarm bells. "Rose," I say slowly, shifting on the cushion so I'm facing her fully. "Who were you talking about? Christina? Did something happen between her and Jackson?"

"No." Her eyes find mine and she grimaces. "God-damn, you really have one of those faces that makes it impossible to lie to you. Matt gave you the perfect nickname."

A shiver coasts down my spine. I'm missing the full puzzle, but I have pieces: Christina fishing about whether Matt and I were living together, her coming into Tullamore yesterday to ask if we would be at the party. I've known her for months, but I can count on one hand the conversations we've had with more than two words.

Unless it wasn't her that wanted to know the answers to those questions.

"The woman with Christina, the brunette," I say, testing the waters. Rose's expression twists, telling me I've hit the nail on the head. "Who is she?"

Rose sighs, giving in. "Melody."

Every muscle in my body tenses. "Melody as in Matt's ex-fiancée?" I ask slowly, and when Rose nods, I frown. "What's she doing here with Christina?"

Rose eyes me carefully, no doubt wondering why I'm not freaking out. On some level, I am. I don't like her being here *at all*, but mostly, I'm just confused.

"They're friends," Rose says. "Melody was the one

who introduced Jackson and Christina. Though I doubt we'll be seeing Christina again after this." The last is muttered.

My short laugh sounds a little too shrill, confirmed by Rose's wince. "Why do you think Melody's here?" When Rose just stares at me, hazel eyes wide, disquiet spreads through me. Dark ripples spread across the surface of my heart, calm since Christmas Eve. "Rose?"

She studies me for another moment, then seems to come to some conclusion. "Do you know where Matt is right now?"

I nod. "Grabbing drinks."

"Find him."

The ripples inside me turn to small waves, sloshing as I rocket to my feet and head for the kitchen.

t took me forever to actually get to the kitchen. Everyone I passed wanted to chitchat, which normally doesn't faze me at all. But all I really want to do is hang with my incredible girlfriend and ignore all these fuckers.

I'm pouring tonic over vodka and ice, daydreaming about sneaking Sophie home before midnight, when a familiar perfume invades my nostrils. It's such an unexpected, shocking sensory trigger that I turn fast, tonic water splashing onto the counter before I right the bottle.

Melody stands before me, a hesitant smile on her face. "Hey, Matt."

For a second, I'm shocked frozen at the sight of her. My brain can't comprehend the fact she's in front of me, familiar cornflower blue eyes on mine. Her hair is darker, a little longer, but other than that, she looks exactly the same. Her dress is short and blue, setting off her eyes and skin.

"You look good," she says.

Weird details and thoughts pop into my still-malfunctioning brain.

Melody's lips are painted with cherry red lipstick that I recognize as her favorite—I remember not liking the taste of it.

Sophie doesn't wear lipstick.

Melody's eyelashes are weirdly long and abnormally full.

Sophie would never wear fake eyelashes. Hers are thick and long all on their own.

"Can we talk?" asks my ex, a flirty smile on her face because she thinks I'm silent for the wrong reasons.

She thinks I'm glad to see her.

The realization helps me find my voice. "No," I say shortly.

She blinks, hurt flashing in her eyes. "Matt," she says in that familiar, pleading tone, "I'm only asking for a few minutes of your time. Let's find somewhere private, okay?"

I lift Sophie's drink and down it in three swallows, then start making her a new one, all the while trying to formulate words that will confer what I want to say without making me sound like a callous asshole.

I don't want to hurt her, but I want her gone.

There's a rising murmur of voices behind me before Julian's voice cuts through the noise. "Melody, you're not welcome here. Kick rocks."

The sudden silence in the kitchen is deafening. A small part of me flinches in sympathy for the woman I used to think I loved, but most of me just feels gratitude and relief that my best friend has my back.

"You heard him," I say, barely glancing at Melody as she gapes at Julian.

"We need to talk," she says to me, digging in because she doesn't actually know how to admit defeat. "You've been ignoring my calls for weeks. Did it occur to you I might have something important to tell you?"

Julian snorts in derision. "Bullshit. Get out. Last warning."

"Before what?" snaps Melody. "What are you going to do, Julian? If you put your hands on me, I'll have you arrested for assault."

Jesus.

There are gasps and shocked mumbles from the room full of silent spectators. Then a new voice pierces the quiet.

"The boys won't have to touch a hair on your head because I'll take out the trash for them."

Every head in the room, mine included, swivels to Kat. She's a tiny woman but scrappy as hell, and from the look on her face, she's not bluffing. Nick stands beside her with a proud look on his face.

And beside Nick is Sophie.

My heart thumps hard as her green eyes shift from Melody to me. The annoyance in them immediately melts into a warmth and love that fills me up and makes me feel invincible.

"Just go," I tell Melody, who's vibrating with rage, her lips pinched.

Her eyes throw sparks as they meet mine. "We're not done."

A light, silvery laugh fills my ears, and the most beautiful woman in the world takes a few steps toward us.

"Yes, you are," Sophie says. "He's mine now."

My gaze drinks in every inch of her. I'm not subtle about the eye-fucking, which I normally try to keep to a minimum in public. A primal part of me growls in approval as Sophie's cheeks flush prettily. So sexy.

So *mine*.

"Nice try," snaps Melody. "You're just the rebound. A passing fetish. I'm his future wife."

My brain stutters, and anger uncoils in my gut. Before I can speak, though, Sophie laughs again.

God, I love her laugh.

I stare at her like the lovestruck idiot I am as she saunters toward me. There's more movement in her hips than usual, a sinuous sensuality that makes my dick stir in my pants and also makes me want to burn out the eyeballs of every man in the room.

She skirts around Melody and tucks herself into my side, her body fitting against mine like a key in a lock. She's the perfect height, with the perfect curves. We fit in a way Melody and I never did, and I see the moment my ex realizes it.

Sophie's words are icicles, clear and sharp. "I'll say it again, since you didn't seem to hear me the first time. He's over you. He's mine. And you're not welcome here."

Melody looks at me with a hint of panic, the first truly genuine emotion I've seen in her tonight. Ignoring Sophie's presence entirely, she opens her mouth and embarrasses herself some more.

"Matt, come on. I just needed some time to think. Don't throw us—everything we had—away. We can get past this. I understand you, remember? I know what you need."

I grimace and shake my head, amazed by her audacity but not really surprised by it. She doesn't care that we have an audience—the only reason we mostly fought in private during our relationship was because I refused to give in to her needling when we were around other people.

"You're delusional," I tell her evenly. "And you know what? So was I for ever thinking we were right for each other. Thank you. *Thank you* for dumping me because I honestly can't imagine how shitty our lives would have been if we'd actually gotten married. I'm done. I'm over you. In fact, I didn't know what love *was* until I met Sophie. And now that I do, I'm never letting it go."

Kat steps up next to us, cracking her knuckles and looking like a fearsomely cute leprechaun. "Any more questions, Melody?"

Christina appears and grabs her arm. "Let's go," she mumbles. Mascara rings her eyes, and across the room I see Jackson staring at her with furious eyes.

And thank fucking God, after a pregnant moment of silence, Melody listens to her friend. The women walk out of the room under a mantel of condemning silence. Kat, Nick, and Julian follow them to make sure they actually leave.

Conversations slowly start back up around us, a mixture of tension-releasing laughter and fervent whispering.

I look down that the goddess in my arms. She smiles up at me.

Fucking radiant.

"What took so long?" she asks, blinking coyly. "I'm thirsty."

I grab her jaw and plant my mouth on hers, delighting in her surprised squeak as I open her lips with mine and drive my tongue into her mouth, branding her in front of everyone with absolutely no shame.

When the lecherous whistles start, I slowly relinquish her face with a final, searing kiss. She blinks up at me, and I grin smugly at the haze of desire in her eyes, her pupils blown wide and surrounded by a thin layer of green.

"I love you," I whisper.

Her smile lights me up. "I love you, too. Can we go home now? I know another way we can celebrate the New Year."

I grab her hand and we haul ass to the car, her giggles playing like music in my ears.

37

 don't plan the phone call, but on a Saturday afternoon in early February, I find myself dialing a number I stored in my phone two months ago.

"This is Agent Faulkner."

My voice comes on the second try. "Hi. My name is Sophie Marshall, and I have information pertaining to a case that's about to go to trial. I don't know if what I have to say will matter much, but I wanted to call."

"I'm glad you did, Sophie. Why don't you tell me your information, and we can decide how to move forward from there."

I take a deep breath. "Steven Yates trafficked me for six months when I was twenty years old. I don't have any evidence, really, except... I'm pretty sure he has scars on his neck. From fingernails."

"And how would you know that?" asks Agent Faulkner, her voice low with interest.

"I put them there when I escaped him."

THE EVIDENCE AGAINST STEVEN—*TED*—IS overwhelming and backed up by hours of damning video and phone recordings, as well as the heartbreaking testimony given by three of his victims, all between the ages of seventeen and twenty-one.

In the end, my own testimony is deemed unnecessary by the prosecution in order to secure a guilty verdict. And though I mull on it for a few weeks, I eventually turn down the offer to read a victim statement at the close of the trial.

Steven Yates is found guilty on all counts and is sentenced to life without the possibility of parole.

Kelly and I drive down to Tacoma after the trial in March, and I meet Agent Faulkner for the first time. Kelly waits in a visitors' area while I'm led into a conference room. There, I come face-to-face with Amy, Vittoria, and Jasmine. Fellow victims. Amazing, powerful young women who put a monster behind bars.

We talk for a long time. I tell them my story. What happened after. What the years since have been like. My highs and lows. What helps; what doesn't. And I tell them what my life is like now.

I tell them the truth.

Not only can we survive, we can thrive.

And we are worthy of real love.

38

On a sunny afternoon in mid-March, I open the final box of my belongings in the downstairs room that's now my art studio. On the outside of the box is scrawled **Art Supplies** in Matt's handwriting.

Pickle's tail flicks against my arm as he passes, wandering and sniffing his way through the room before curling up by the window where a shaft of late afternoon sunlight hits the wooden floorboards. It's an unusually warm day, and the window is cracked to let in a spring breeze.

I open the flaps of the box and promptly burst out laughing.

Lying atop a short stack of sketchbooks is the old GQ Magazine with Matt on the cover. Scrawled over his ripped abs are words in Sharpie marker.

PROPERTY OF SOPHIE MARSHALL

His signature is below it.

"What are you laughing about in here?" His footsteps come up behind me, then he sees what I'm holding and chuckles. "Ahh, you finally opened the box."

I look up at him, laughing anew at the self-satisfied smirk on his face. He nods to the box, his grin widening. "Keep looking."

I pull out the three sketchbooks, groaning as I recognize them. Sure enough, a few page flips are all it takes for me to want to die of mortification. The oldest one is at least five years old, and he's still the central subject matter.

"You were obsessed with me for years, Dollface."

He sounds so fucking happy about it, I can't even hang on to my embarrassment. I grab the magazine and sketchbooks in one arm and wave my other hand at him. "Help me up. Or is your head too inflated now?"

He laughs and pulls me effortlessly from the floor. I turn and head for the bookshelf where my other, newer sketchbooks sit. He follows, his hands sneaking around my waist and under my shirt, hot palms against my bare skin.

I slide the books and magazine onto the shelf, then

turn and wind my arms around his neck. "Are you packed?"

He lowers his face to my neck, breathing deeply. "Let's just stay home."

Home.

The word floats peacefully through my mind, lifting my lips into a smile. "I'm pretty sure Breaking Giants needs their guitarist for South by Southwest."

"But Pickle will miss us," he murmurs, soft lips dragging over my jaw.

I laugh. "He will, but he tolerates Kelly. He'll be fine. Now go pack because our flight is at the ass crack of dawn tomorrow."

He huffs in defeat. "Fine, we'll go, but only if you do something for me first."

I roll my eyes. "I'm not giving you a blow job right now, Matthew."

His eyes widen in surprise, then he laughs and grabs me to plant a kiss on my lips. "Maybe not right now, but I bet I can persuade you later."

I smack his shoulder, but concede with a grin, "Yeah, your odds are pretty good. So, what do you need me to do? If it's helping you make dinner, the answer is no way. I've been in here all day and I'm exhausted."

We've made a habit of cooking together at least three times a week, and I'd be lying if I said I didn't enjoy it.

Matt teaching me to cook is both fun and surprisingly erotic. At least once a week, we don't actually finish cooking and end up ordering delivery hours later.

He smiles. "Nope. Dinner's already ready. I just need your help in the backyard for a sec."

Before I can ask for more details, he grabs my hand and tugs me down the hallway, past the kitchen, and through the living room.

"After you," he says, holding the back door open for me to pass.

I take a step outside, and my fingers go numb and slip from his.

Our families are gathered on the grass by the giant oak tree. Strings of lights sweep through the air overhead from the tree's branches to the house, and there's a long table on the grass, beautifully set with a white tablecloth, vases of flowers, and about a dozen dishes of food.

"What is this?" I whisper-hiss at Matt. "Did I forget something important?"

"No." His throat moves as he swallows, but his gaze stays steady on mine. "I snuck them through the side gate. Our moms and sisters set everything up."

So that's why he checked on me a dozen times in the last hour—to make sure I didn't leave the room while they were working in the backyard.

My stomach tumbles, a queer lightness tingling in my limbs.

I glance back at my mom and Beka, who wave at me with shit-eating grins. Matt's mom and sister are only marginally less enthused, both of them smiling happily. Even my brothers and Matt's dad are smiling, though Josh looks on the verge of maniacal laughter; he knows I hate surprises.

I spin back to Matt but gasp as I realize he's on one knee before me. He's not smiling as he gazes up at me, however; he looks terrified.

Oh my God.

His face blurs until I blink away a film of tears. On the verge of laughter, or possibly hysteria, I whisper in a strangled voice, "Matthew?"

He grabs my hands in his, which are warm and just the slightest bit clammy. "Sophie Anne Marshall, I love you with my whole heart, which I didn't even realize wasn't whole until I met you. I know this is fast. I know you want to kick me in the neck right now. But I couldn't wait anymore. You're everything I want and need, and I never want to be apart from you. Will you marry me?"

Tears spill down my cheeks. I don't want to kick him. Not even a little bit.

I want to love him forever.

"Yes. *Yes.* Of course I'll marry you."

Our families raise a cheer and Matt surges to his feet, lips claiming mine for a heated few seconds before he pulls something from his pocket. Something that sparkles with green fire in the fading daylight.

"Holy shit," I gasp as he slips the ring onto my finger. It fits perfectly.

A sob bursts out of me.

"You don't like it? God, I'm sorry. We can go shopping together. I thought you wouldn't want a diamond, but—oof."

I collide with his chest, yanking his face down to mine to kiss him. Then I kiss him again. Between kisses, I say, "It's perfect. Absolutely breathtaking. I love emeralds. I love you."

Tension drains from his body. "Thank God. Fuck, I love you so much. I'm so glad you said yes. I'll spend the rest of my life making sure you never regret it."

His hand slips around the back of my neck, angling my face to deepen our kiss. His other palm strokes down my back and grips my hip, pulling me soundly against him.

"Okay, okay!" cries Josh. "Heading toward PG-13 here!"

The backyard fills with laughter.

MATT ISN'T the only one with a surprise. I was planning on saving my news for after South by Southwest, but after we say goodbye to our families, I run upstairs to fetch the little box hidden in the back of our closet.

Biting my lip on a smile, I put the box on his pillow, then head to the shower.

My wait isn't long. I'm rinsing shampoo from my hair when the bathroom door slams open and Matt stalks across the bathroom toward me.

"*Dollface,*" he growls. His hand thumps on the shower door, a plastic stick with a purple cap on the end trapped between his palm and the glass.

I struggle to keep a straight face. "What's that?"

To my horror, his eyes redden and fill with tears. I wrench open the shower door and he steps in, fully clothed, to gather me against his chest.

"Matthew," I say, running my hands over his hair. "Are you okay? I'm sorry, I thought—"

"You're pregnant," he whispers hoarsely. He leans back, holding my face between his hands like I'm fragile art. His eyes scan mine. "How?"

I wince. "Apparently, birth control is only ninety-three percent effective if you don't take it at the exact same time every day. Or if you accidentally skip one—like I did—even if you take two the next day. I messed up. And now we're having a baby." I say the last tentatively, hope an ember in my chest waiting for oxygen only he can give it.

And he does.

"This is the best day of my life." He presses his lips to my forehead and a shudder runs down his body. "A baby. We're having a baby."

His lips find mine, grazing gently before pressing deeper. His teeth graze my lower lip and I open for his tongue, melting against his soaking wet shirt. He's still holding me carefully, his hands gentle on my bare waist.

"Matt," I huff. "I won't break."

"Thank fuck," he breathes, then tears off his shirt. His wet jeans follow, thumping heavily to the ground, and then I'm lifted against the cool tiles of the wall. One arm braced behind me, he leans back, his other hand splaying across my abdomen. "Hi, tiny tadpole. Your daddy loves you."

"Ruining the moment," I grumble, but I'm smiling, so filled with joy I'm surprised I'm not glowing.

Matt's smile fades, his features sharpening as that questing hand lowers and cups between my legs, his thumb circling gently against my clit, long fingers playing in wetness that has nothing to do with the shower spray. A flush moves over my body, my hips rocking, my nails digging into his shoulders.

"Stop teasing," I say, nipping at his jaw.

We groan in shared relief as he sinks inside me, the sounds tangling with our tongues. Matt's hips move in steady, body-wrecking thrusts, his arms the safest, most secure place in the world.

"Mine, all mine," he murmurs against my cheek, "Mmm, I can feel how close you are. Tight, hot, and dripping. That's it, baby. Let go. Oh, fuck yes—"

I climax with a raw cry, my teeth digging into his shoulder. His breath stutters, a gasping growl in his throat as he follows me off the edge into still, peaceful waters.

EPILOGUE

SIX YEARS LATER

'**ve** never seen so many kids in my life. The backyard is overflowing with little hellions in various stages of sugar madness, running around the (safely fenced) pool, jumping in a giant rented bounce house, stuffing their faces with pizza and candy, and squealing as they wiggle like worms on the massive play structure that took Julian, Nick, Jackson, and me ten freaking hours to build.

My gaze roams as I take it all in, then narrows when I spy the Tiny Trio of Evil at the back of the bounce house near the controls. The oldest, a boy with dark, curly hair, is the definite ringleader, his hands gesticulating wildly as he lays out the steps toward world—or birthday party—domination.

I'm somewhat mollified to see the blond little girl shaking her head, her arms crossed and a cute frown on her face. The sparkly Birthday Girl tiara she wears slips a little to the side; I smirk as the dark-haired boy immediately straightens it even as the argument continues. The final villain is a redheaded boy, the youngest of the trio. He listens avidly as his heroes go back and forth. He'll side with the girl; he always does.

"That's not suspicious or anything," says Julian dryly, settling in the chair beside me. "What's my little menace up to?"

"Pretty sure he's trying to convince *my* little menace to turn off the bounce house with all the kids still in it," I supply, then nod to Nick, who's striding their way with an expression of feigned intensity; I know he's laughing inside. "Nick's got it."

Julian chuckles. "You were just going to let them do it?"

I shrug and stroke my fingertips across the downy head of the four-month-old strapped to my chest. "Booger's nap was more important."

"I can't believe you still call him Booger."

I grin. "I seem to remember you calling Wilder Beebo for the first year of his life."

Julian smirks. "True." In a softer voice, he asks, "How's Sophie doing?"

My gaze follows his to my wife. She's chatting with Rose, Kat, and Jackson's wife, Alicia. As usual, my chest warms as I drink her in; she'll always be the most beautiful woman in the world to me. Each year that passes, my love for her grows.

There's a serious undercurrent to Julian's question, however; one I can't ignore.

"A lot better," I say, and thankfully, it's true.

Postpartum has been no joke. We found out pretty fast that Sophie isn't one of those lucky women who grow humans with little or no adverse emotional effects. Both pregnancies were hard—during and after—especially since we lost our first pregnancy at twelve weeks. When Sophie got pregnant again the following winter, we were overjoyed and yet, neither of us had ever experienced that kind of fear.

My gaze veers to Eva Marie—our rainbow baby, named after our maternal grandmothers. A smile curves over my mouth at the sight of her on the new swing set that was christened with the sweat and tears of grown men.

She squeals, her face alight. My hair; her mother's eyes.

"Higher, WhyWhy, higher!"

Wilder complies with an eye roll for the nickname he hates but my kid won't quit using. Nick and Kat's son, Riley, is on the other swing doing his best to pump his skinny legs and catch up with Eva's trajectory.

"We're going to be in a world of pain with that crew when they hit puberty," murmurs my best friend, a knowing smile on his face.

I hum in agreement, dropping a kiss on my son's soft head. I can't say I'm looking forward to Eva growing too big to want her dad's cuddles and piggyback rides, but the truth of the matter is I have no complaints.

Looking around the backyard, my gaze snags again on the center of my world. Sophie's eyes meet mine, her smile shifting, becoming the one that belongs to me and reflects the same love I feel for her.

I once thought this exact day—kids running around, my friends and family with me—would represent the pinnacle of success and happiness in my life.

But it's *her*.

She's the dream that came true.

THE END

I hope you enjoyed Sophie and Matt's love story. If you have a minute, please consider leaving a brief review.

xo,

L

ACKNOWLEDGMENTS

I saw a Facebook post recently by an author asking if people actually read the Acknowledgments, and I wasn't surprised to find that many readers don't. I don't blame them; this part of the book is more for us. A final stamp on a book so we can look back years later and remember who we were, what our lives were like, when we wrote the story.

This particular book was written faster than any novel in my career. Some days, it felt like the words barely paused as they came from my subconscious to the page. I would reread chapters and truly question whether or not I'd been possessed, having little to no memory of writing them.

That said, Sophie and Matt have a very, very special place in my heart. I absolutely fell in love with both of them, and it was a joy to return to the world of *Breaking Giants* and check in with Rose, Julian, and the rest of the crew.

Special thanks go to PJ, paramedic-extraordinaire and best friend of my late husband, Don. That scene with Beka—though brief—was especially hard for me to write due to my own trauma, and just as PJ held my hand on the worst day of my life, he held my hand during the writing of that chapter as I navigated my own emotions and how to realistically portray what Beka and Sophie experienced in those taut minutes.

Oh, and PJ wanted me to tell you he's available to the romance author community for interviews and/or cover modeling. ;)

As always, thank you to my beta readers Steph, Dawn, and Danielle and my editor, Emily Lawrence.

Finally, in no particular order, thanks go to: Nicole, Jessica, Lacee, Dave, and the light of my life, my daughter, Stella.

Until the next one...

xo,

Laura

ALSO BY L.M. HALLORAN

FORBIDDEN ROMANCE

The Dark Before Light

The Fall Before Flight

The Muse

ROCKSTAR ROMANCE

Breaking Giants

Breaking Silence

Loving Wild (2025)

SMALL TOWN

Room for Us

Time for Us

DARK ROMANTIC SUSPENSE

Double Vision

Perfect Vision

The Golden Hour

Art of Sin *(Illusions Duet #1)*

Sin of Love *(Illusions Duet #2)*

BILLIONAIRE ROMANCE

The Reluctant Socialite

The Reluctant Heiress

. . .

URBAN FANTASY / PNR

AS LAURA HALL

THE WHITE ORDER

Wellspring

Scroll of Secrets

THE ASCENSION SERIES

Ascension

Reckoning

Unraveling

Rebirth

Tribulation

Revelation

ABOUT THE AUTHOR

When not writing or reading, the author can be found chasing her daughter. Some of her favorite things are puzzles, podcasts, and small dogs that resemble Ewoks.

Home is Portland, Oregon.

lmhalloran.com